Strange Liberty

Johannes T. Evans

Salvo Caine, a young man cursed with a magically sapping touch, is convicted of manslaughter and dispatched to an island prison. Once there, he's offered limited freedom — and affection — by the cold and manipulative prison warden, Guillaume Villiers.

Rated M, 27.5k, dark fantasy with some M/M dark romance on the side. Good bit of age gap sexiness, and some medical and care-giving kink as well.

All depicted sex and intimate scenes are fully consensual, barring one foiled attempt at assault, which is only a few paragraphs.

Note CWs for the expected violence of the prison system; past chronic illness and child neglect; threats of and discussion of sexual violence; traumatic death; power struggles and fucked-up dynamics.

Strange Liberty is a work of fiction created from the author's imagination. Any resemblance to living persons, living or dead, or resemblance to actual events, places, or names is purely coincidental.

Strange Liberty

He arrives in the middle of the fucking night, and Redford leans up against the open trap, watching as the guards come in. They're all soaked through from the fucking rain, must have had a bad boat trip over – he looks fucking tiny in between all the guards coming in with him. Half a dozen guards would normally be the standard to transport a whole coach of new meat, but they always put a whole unit alongside this sort of inmate, just in case.

When the guards part, Redford gets a good look at him, slim and slight with a thick cloud of hair and very big eyes. His ankles and his wrists are cuffed, chains running between the four points and making him move slow.

He stumbles and collapses to the floor on his knees and elbows, making the chains rattle, and Redford can't even hear the names the guards call him or the things they snap at him over the roar of everybody else watching him come in.

Already, he'd been able to hear the quieter talk and laughter up and down the rows of cells, prisoners talking about him – now, on the floor with his ass in the air, that's too much not to react to.

"That arse looks like it'll bruise nice and easy!" he hears Rand call from the floor below, and he hears other jeers and compliments – about the lad's backside, about his thighs, how tight his boycunt'll be, how pretty his lips are, how they'll be happy to show him what real men get up to behind bars.

It's always like this, with the cuffed mages.

Half the men in this prison have suffered at the hands of magic-users like them, and even if they hadn't, the attitudes they come in with are enough to hate them over. Even the big, more muscular ones get this sort of intimidation – they're usually arrogant sorts, used to relying on their magic instead of any strength or agility, and with their magic dampened, they end up pretty easy to push around, and they deserve it, too.

Haughty, over-educated, always acting like they're too good to be in here with the rest of them.

Redford is the first to get at him in the morning when he comes out of the new arrivals' cell. He doesn't look like he's slept, dark bags under his eyes, his lips chapped and bitten bruised, and he doesn't meet a single man's eye as he nervously steps out of his cell.

Red shoves him up against the wall, and he drags in a hitched breath, his big eyes going wide – Red's belly is flattening him back against the stone, and he can feel him trembling, feel how warm he is. Red leans in and breathes on the side of his neck, blows air over his ear, but he doesn't say anything.

"How long are you in for, sweetheart?" Red asks softly. "You even know what deep shit you're in?"

The new meat's gaze is fixed on Red's upper chest instead of his face.

There's a clicking of a tongue behind him, and Redford steps back from the new inmate, making him drop like a weight. He stands back and straight to attention as he glances back at the warden, who's standing in the centre of the corridor, leaning on his cane.

"Warden Villiers," Red says.

"I wish you weren't so quick to make new acquaintances at times, Mr Redford," Villiers says mildly, and Red grins at him. "In my office, Mr Caine, if you would."

Caine cringes, looks anxiously between Redford and Villiers both, and when he looks up to meet Red's eyes for the first time, there's something pleading in them. It only lasts a second, and then he's trailing after Villiers down the corridor.

Red watches them go, and hums thoughtfully to himself before he heads to eat.

* * *

Salvo shivers as he follows up the stairs to Villiers' office, feels the chill on the back of his neck, insinuating itself under his skin. Villiers moves slowly, leaning heavily on his cane for the support it can give him as they ascend – he speeds up a little once they're on even ground. Salvo risks looking up at the older man as they move, looks at how thin he is – even thinner than Salvo is himself, pointy and angular under his black suit, which is narrowly tailored.

He wears boots instead of shoes, although they're not like the guards' boots. These barely make any noise at all on the smooth lacquered floors, and they come in tight to the ankle and the foot.

A guard opens the door for Villiers, and Villiers nods his head for Salvo to step into the room ahead of him.

After crossing the threshold, painfully aware of Villiers' gaze on the back of his neck, he goes to stand in the middle of the room, in front of Villiers' desk.

It's warmer in here than in the prison proper, a fire crackling in the hearth, which has a firmly bolted set of guards around it and a very small trap on the front with only just enough space to reach in and move coals and kindling.

"Thank you, Rusk, you're relieved."

"... Sir? But he's, um..."

"I have a firm handle on our new addition, Rusk, I don't need your assistance."

Villiers closes the door behind the guard, and Salvo hears his bootsteps recede down the corridor.

Salvo swallows as Villiers slides the lock across and then moves into the room. He sets his cane in a bucket with an umbrella to one side, and Salvo watches the way he favours his good leg as he moves across the room, laying his hands on the side of a bookshelf, then on his desk, to support himself.

"Are you frightened?" Villiers asks.

Salvo doesn't know what the correct answer is, and says nothing.

Villiers goes on, as if he'd said yes, "I would be too. You heard the baying of those jackals out there as you arrived – fresh meat, they called you. And those men are passionate carnivores."

Salvo presses his lips together, gripping his fingers against one another in front of his belly, and he risks a glance up at Villiers' face. It's a somewhat handsome face, although severely featured – his eyes are a dark blue, his eyebrows thick and dark in colour, his upper lip very thin, his lower lip thicker. He's got very thin skin, and in places Salvo can see the blue show through of his veins, especially on the side of his neck where his throat adjoins his head.

His face droops on one side.

"You had a stroke?" Salvo asks. He doesn't mean to ask the question – it comes out of his mouth unbidden, and when Villiers smirks at him, the smile is lopsided, stronger on the left side of his face than his right.

"That's right," he says quietly. "You were a nurse, yes?"

"No," says Salvo. "I'm just a care assistant."

"You didn't want to pursue nursing?"

"Didn't have the marks for university. I was looking for an apprenticeship, but it's hard to get a place." He frowns, and looks down at the rug beneath their feet, an antique thing with a dark green and blue pattern. "Won't be able to get one now."

"Why ever not?"

"DBS check."

"Magical crimes aren't always included on mundane criminal records," Villiers says mildly. "It's decided on a case-by-case basis upon the prisoner's release."

Salvo doesn't say anything, but he does exhale, feeling at the same time relieved, and also as if a trap is being laid for him.

"Why am I here?" he asks.

"I think you should know that by now," says Villiers snidely, and Salvo presses his lips together, clenching his jaw to keep from snapping back, because that *is* a trap.

"Why am I in your *office*, sir?"

"Well, that's rather up to you," Villiers says, his voice softer now. His boots still don't make any sound as he comes out from behind his desk, and Salvo doesn't move as he watches the shadow of the other man in his peripheral vision, feels him come closer. The older man's breath is warm on the back of his neck, making Salvo shiver and have to resist leaning back into him – he smells very faintly of coffee, mostly smells of shaving foam and camphor oil. "Why would you like to be in my office, Mr Caine?"

"I don't understand."

"Young man, this is a prison filled to the brim with hardened criminals. Many of them, despite being so inclined, haven't known the touch of a woman since they were incarcerated – pretty thing as you are, I'm sure you'll do in a pinch."

Salvo doesn't say anything, but he can't stop himself from letting out a short, abortive sound when Villiers lays his hands on his shoulders, grips them, presses his narrow thumbs into the tension on the back of his neck. He's so unused to being touched, and it feels painfully good, makes his skin feel like it's singing – he leans back into it, and he lets out another small noise, this one of loss, as Villiers steps away and releases him.

"Your fellow inmates will make use of you," Villiers says, "and short of fucking you, I expect they'll push you about a bit, bruise you, hurt you here and there. You're an easy prospect to bully, with your magic dampened and that protection stripped from you. Do you want that?"

"To be bullied? No, I don't think so."

"And to have them fuck you?"

Salvo thinks of the noise it had made when he'd come in and they'd all been shouting and banging on the walls, laughing, how loud it had been. It had been... overwhelming.

He's spent a long time avoiding crowds, groups of people, avoiding anyone who might be forward in trying to touch him, speak to him, want to fuck him. His whole body aches with want, but not for that.

"Are the guards meant to let them?" Salvo asks.

"No," Villiers says. "Any guard I caught abusing an inmate, I'd have punished – any guard permitting it, I'd punish myself. The so-minded inmates tend to hide this sort of thing, of course, and guards rarely advertise it either."

"That sounds like an excuse."

"It is – but a true one. I don't have enough guards to watch each man twenty-four hours a day, though, or even just the pretty ones who might prove a temptation."

"Am I pretty?"

"In here? You're a vision."

"You're suggesting something. An alternative."

"Offering something, rather. Protection, if you'd like it."

"From other inmates?"

"You'll be with the general population through most of the day – work duties, recreation outdoors. But I can arrange particular bathing and bedding arrangements for you."

"Bedding," Salvo repeats.

"Quite," the warden says. "A bed to lay your head on, no cellmates, no risk."

"Except from you."

"From *me*? Young man, what risk do you think I pose you? Look at me – an infirm old man, no risk to anybody at all."

Salvo looks up at Villiers' face again, at the sly expression there, the amusement writ in his glittering eyes and lopsided smile.

"What do you want, if not sex?"

"I'm offering out of the goodness of my heart," Villiers says with utter insincerity, so transparent about it that Salvo almost marvels. "We both know you're not a criminal like the majority of my other charges."

"I'm a murderer."

"A manslaughterer," Villiers corrects him. His tone is surprisingly kind as he says, "I actually tried to refuse you, insist you go to a more appropriate institution than this one, but the decision was out of my hands."

Salvo looks down at his own hands, gripping tightly at one another, tighter now. His knuckles hurt, and are going white from the clenching in his hands. "You're not going to fuck me?"

"No. Have you had sex before?"

Salvo nods.

"Consensually?"

Salvo hesitates, not certain how to answer, but then he nods.

"Hm, well. Nonetheless, no."

Salvo shifts his hands, and he feels the weight of the two metal bands around each of his wrists. When he'd been brought in last night, a chain had run between them and two more round his ankles to keep him halfway bound, but they'd taken most of that away when they'd left him to his cell. Now, the cuffs just sit around each of his wrists, simple bracelets of silver. He can see the sheen of the magic in them when he looks at them directly, watch the pulse of it through the metal in rhythm with his heartbeat – in rhythm with the magic inside him.

"You didn't have to come to prison to have those fitted," Villiers tells him. "You wouldn't even have had to have them commissioned – any good doctor would have provided them free of charge."

Salvo opens his mouth, closes it. "There is a gnawing hunger in me," he whispers after a pause. "These cuffs prevent me from harming anybody, true, but they also prevent latent magic from flowing through me. I eat, but I starve; I drink, but I thirst. Ever since they snapped shut around my limbs my bones began to ache."

"That hunger is part of your penance, then," Villiers says, and Salvo closes his eyes, but nods his head. "I read the statement you gave at your trial, that you wish you'd chosen differently."

"Wouldn't you have?"

Villiers limps around the table and sinks down into his chair, making it creak, and Salvo automatically sits to keep his downcast eyes from being so close to Villiers' face, to keep from keeping his stare.

"I thought it would be enough," Salvo murmurs. "Separating myself from magical life, magical society, living and working with mundies. That I could keep myself intact, and still live."

"You crossed paths with your victim by happenstance, I take it?"

"He wouldn't have touched me, only he recognised me," Salvo says. "Recognised my father's features in mine. He caught my hand, and it was..."

He thinks of it often. Every day, every night, when he sleeps, when he wakes – it's impossible not to think about. He thinks of how it was as though his flesh came suddenly alive after being halfway to comatose for so long, as though lightning were alive under his skin, sizzling out of his veins. He recalls craving more of it, the reflexive need to be closer, much closer, to sate the painful hunger in him.

"He didn't know to— he didn't think to push me off or away. He didn't know that... He laughed, was delighted, and he embraced me back when I kissed him on the cheek. I had effectively been fasting for years, near to a decade. I leeched from him all he had before I knew what I was doing."

"A horrible way to die, I'm informed," Villiers says. "To have the magic wrenched from you, sapped from your very cells – like having the blood bled from you all at once."

"He didn't have time to scream," Salvo says. "But yes, it hurt him a great deal."

"At least it was quick."

"I fail to see a silver lining."

"A guard will collect you when it's time for lights out," Villiers says. "Off you go."

Salvo silently nods his head, and as he leaves the room, can't help feeling he's made some sort of deal with a devil, going along with the offer as given.

* * *

Red watches the new mage as he comes back from the stairs, not with the warden this time – Villiers is a freak of some proportions, always likes the strong mages, always likes the trim and pretty ones.

"He used to be an assassin, you know," he says when Caine finally comes down onto the main floor, and Caine glances his way, but doesn't let his gaze flicker all the way up to Red's face. He stands there with his hands clasped in front of him, silent. "Villiers."

"How the fuck was he an assassin with a bum leg?" asks Rosen next to him, and Pike grips the back of his neck as Redford laughs.

"He *used* to be an assassin," Red repeats. "Killed people the world over – then he had a stroke, couldn't hack it anymore."

"'Cause of his leg."

"It's not just the leg and the facial droop," says Pike. His gaze is on Rosen's neck as he keeps rubbing his thumb into the base of it. Red can see the mark higher up on Rosen's throat where Pike must have bitten him last night.

Caine has drifted closer to them, albeit without saying a word.

"Strokes on different sides of the body damage different parts of the brain," says Pike. It's easy to forget, what with his thick Birmingham accent and how fucking dirty he is half the time, that he's an educated man. He might be a drug trafficker who does twenty kinds of violence in an average month, but he knows a lot about animals, plants, and mushrooms, and he knows a good bit of folk medicine his mother taught him too. "Difficulties with language, or with writing, mathematics... But that can include differences in personality. He was a wild man before – he's cold now. Collected, but cold, cautious."

"You speak as though you know personally," says Caine, but he doesn't lift his eyes up. "You don't look old enough for all that."

"I'm not so old," says Pike, and Red watches the way he looks at Caine, the way his eyes rove over the new meat's body. He's not interested in sex in this case, of course – he likes a man for the blood inside him, and with a skinny little thing like Caine, there's not much blood to spare, even without the taint Pike's complained before that the cuffs leave on the stuff when you tap the barrel.

"He was killing into his forties," Redford says. "He's fifty-six now, had the stroke years back. Came to be warden here after getting out of rehab."

"His personality used to be different?" Caine asks.

"Why?" Red asks mildly. "You like his personality now?"

Caine might not speak much, but he's got a nice voice. It's stronger, warmer, than Red would have thought from the looks of him, so slim with his big brown eyes, the fluff of his dark curls around his head.

Caine doesn't answer, so Red reaches out and grips him by the hair, slides his fingers through the curls and tightens his hold experimentally – Caine goes loose and breathless immediately, his lips parting, his eyes widening. A blush darkens his cheeks and his knees look loose. He doesn't try to drag away, doesn't seem to be following Redford's hand out of reflex, either – he's up on his toes, pushing up into more of the touch.

"Leave the kid alone, Redford!" barks Cornell from the other side of the hall, and Red lets him go.

"You have a heartbeat like a mouse's," Pike says. He's a freak and all, and doesn't make any attempt to hide it – Caine, to his credit, doesn't let it put him off. "Quiet and fast."

"What are you in for?" Rosen asks, and Caine's eyes flicker up to him. Rosen's smaller than he is, and he looks Rosen in the eyes easier than he does Red or Villiers – with Rosen, Caine can look down into his face.

"You first," he says.

"I killed a guy," says Rosen, and Caine stares at him, his eyes widening further, his lips parting.

"You did?" he asks, and Rosen laughs before Pike slaps him upside the head.

"Theft," Rosen says, chuckling. "Cars. A bus. A train, they charged me for, but I didn't steal that."

"Only 'cause you couldn't drive it off the tracks," Redford says, and Rosen laughs. "Now you."

"I killed a man," says Caine, and Rosen laughs again.

Caine doesn't. He stands there with his hands still clasped in that way he has, still. He looks like a little statuette of a saint.

"Oh, shit," says Rosen. "He have it coming?"

Caine's gaze flickers to Red's chest, but not all the way up to his face. "No," he says. He looks like he's sad about it, like he regrets it, but then his eyes shift upwards and he meets Red's gaze, something in Caine's face goes hard. "Do you?"

Red grins down at him, and as soon as he shows his teeth, Caine retreats, turning away – one of the guards takes him through his paces, shows him around the place, tells him the schedule.

The evening time, though, he disappears.

He doesn't stay in the new transplants' cell and doesn't get moved in with someone else's either – Red wonders if he's been put in confinement on his own, all the better to keep him "safe", but when he's passing Beck Virgo's cell a little before lights out, Beck tells him.

"Saw him out of the window," he murmurs as Red passes him a cigarette through the trap. "Trailing behind Villiers like a fucking puppy."

"Huh," Redford murmurs, and thinks on that as he continues down the corridor.

* * *

The guest bedroom in Villiers' lodge, separate from the prison proper, is modest, warm, and comfortable.

It's nothing like the cell he'd been in, nor the cells that he'd seen in the prison – each has rather narrow bunks, thin mattresses, thin blankets, battered pillows. The sheets are cheap, made of crisp white cloth, and they're all laundered en masse in the basement, but not with particularly forgiving products. A prison bed is not meant to be a place of comfort or ease, after all, nor the cells themselves.

This guest bedroom is made to serve one man, a lush double bed in the middle of the room, the bedspread red and silken, the fabric smooth under his fingers. There's a chair and a desk to the side of the room, and Salvo stands with his hands rested on the desk, looking out over the hill.

The window doesn't open, is just a set of wide panes, but at least there are no bars. Salvo can see the old stone sprawl of the prison over the island, can see the forestry either side; in the distance, he can see the pier, a boat tethered and waiting. The waters are choppy this evening, and although he can't hear the wind through the thick glazed glass, he can see the trees whipping one way and the other.

"Comfortable enough for you?" asks Villiers, standing in the doorway.

He's undressed, and Salvo stares at his body – he's still wearing his suit trousers, but instead of his boots he's wearing crushed velvet slippers, and belted over his chest he's wearing a fine silk brocade smoking jacket, green and gold. If he's wearing a shirt underneath, it has a low collar or none at all – where the smoking jacket is open, Salvo can see the edges of Villiers' collarbone, the hollows in it; further down, he can see the curls of hair on his chest.

Salvo's hands twitch at his sides, and his mouth feels dry.

"Yes," he says. "Yes, thank you. Is there some hidden consequence about to be sprung on me?"

"Am I going to clamber into bed with you, you mean?" Villiers asks, arching one eyebrow. "No, young man, I'm going to sleep in my own bed, where I belong. This door will be locked as I depart – you have your own bathroom, where you might pursue your evening ablutions, take a shower, and so forth. Any items you purchase from the commissary, books from the library, items you receive by post once your approval comes through, you might keep all these things here in your bedroom.

"In the event prisoners are confined to their cells during day time, you will be escorted to my office, whereupon you will either rest there with me or be brought here and locked in. Beyond such extenuating circumstances, however, you will not be able to return to your room here in the course of a day – you might want to keep that in mind when you consider what to bring out with you, your books, writing implements, and so on."

"Yes, sir," Salvo says. "Do you want me to be raped, sir?"

"What a curious question," Villiers says, his blue eyes dark and stormy, his smile still dangerously sly. "Why ever would you ask it? I've made rather unorthodox choices if my desire was to have you victimised, bringing you here, isolated from the other prisoners, or even the guards."

"I've never been at home with unorthodoxy," Salvo says honestly, looking cautiously at the other man. "It strikes me as unpredictable."

"I'm predictable enough," Villiers murmurs. "I'm sure you'll have the way of it quite soon."

"They said you used to be very different, the other prisoners. Before you had a stroke."

"What would they know of it?"

"Only hearsay, I suppose."

"Hearsay, yes. Hearsay, and rumour."

"Is it true?"

"Does it matter?"

"Why wouldn't it?"

"If I am different than I was before my stroke, the change is now permanent. What does it matter to you, young man, if I was different before now?"

"Aren't you interested in how different I was, before I became an inmate here?" Salvo asks.

It's the right question, and posed right too – Villiers stares at him, his expression retaining exactly the same slightly smug expression it had before, and then he exhales, smiles, adjusts his grip on his cane. He seems satisfied.

"We've plenty of time to get to know one another, Mr Caine. And many evenings ahead of us to do so."

"Is that the purpose of my being here?" Salvo asks, and Villiers chuckles quietly, pulling the door closed and locking it behind him.

Salvo takes to his bed and sleeps well despite it all.

* * *

Salvo Caine is a funny sort.

Red doesn't see any problem with some mages being raped when they come into the nick, the ones that deserve it – there are men in this place who've spent all their years chained or controlled by very powerful or just quite sadistic sorcerers, and it's more than a little cathartic for them to take out all that pain on whoever the fuck comes in chained and manacled. They go all their days able to hurt anybody they like, able to get away with all sorts, and when they finally get done for it, the tables are turned on them, and suddenly the scum under their feet get to turn around and give them the same shit back.

Red's been at the mercy of a lot of men like that, and not raped, no, but he's had them fuck him over here and there – and more importantly, he's had them fuck over Red's lads, had them try to avoid paying out injured workers or get out of insurance, or even try and play silly buggers with younger lads Red has under his purview, apprentices and that.

Rape is the least of what they deserve, when that's how they carry on, thinking they can get away with it. It's not nice, no, and maybe it's not really moral, but he couldn't give a fuck.

Morals and ethics are limited in a place like this – when you live out your nights and half your days in a little grey box with bars on the door, there's no fucking space for them. Red himself has never gone in much for rape – it doesn't turn him on like it does some of the others, and even without his ED to contend with, he's got a job concentrating on keeping his cock hard if he's wrestling with whoever's underneath him in the process, but it's not because he cares that it's fucking *wrong*, any more than punching a man's lights out is wrong. If he deserves it, if he's fucking earned it, who cares?

But in all honesty, he doesn't much go in for men at all, although there's as little room here for choice as there is morals and ethics – when he fucks a lad in here, it's typically the ones like Salvo Caine. Round in the face, slim or slight but with a bit of plumpness to them, enough softness to sink into – his hair is soft too, all fluffy with those thick dark curls, and with his big fucking eyes, he looks girlish enough, even without turning him around.

In all honesty though, soft as it might fucking make him, it's not the sex he misses – he wasn't married, no, but he had a few regular women he'd take up with depending on where he was working, and it was the sharing a bed he missed, the feeling of someone sleeping beside him, smelling her perfume, touching her hair.

Caine is an odd duck, and it's not like he could be mistaken for a girl to glance at him, at the shape of his shoulders or his body, the way he moves. He's not a very big lad – he's not skinny and has good flesh on him, but there's a delicacy to him, subtly pear-shaped and average height, most of the plushness around his middle and his thighs, less on his chest and about his shoulders. He walks very carefully, like he's nervous of making any noise at all.

Red's not surprised when he hears someone talking about it, about what he's in for – it's not as if Caine's going to be the only lad in the nick for something that wasn't his fucking fault, something that basically amounted to a twist of fate or an accident, but that doesn't mean he has to like it, has to approve of it.

All his life, he's made certain trade-offs – as a lad when he was training up for the glass trade, he remembers learning how to fiddle the books from the out, remembers laughing conversations as they bought sand or panes or whatever else, about how much one thing was and how much they'd write down it was. Smuggling had been a pretty natural extension of it all, once he was running his own business, bringing things in from abroad and secreting the illicit alongside the legit.

It had been getting into the latter that had got him fucking pinched, working in with the Pikes out of Lashton and trafficking too much in drugs and highs for it to be ignored or overlooked.

It wasn't that he hadn't *cared*, per se – that'd be fucking stupid, it's not like he enjoys it here – but he had felt the weight getting bigger and bigger, felt the other shoe getting too heavy *not* to drop, felt the shadow of it all over his head. When he'd come home to find the coppers going through his house and the pig leaning against the wall with the warrant in his hands, at the same time as the pit had gone out of his stomach and nausea had come clawing up his throat, he'd even felt a bit of relief.

Not out of guilt – who'd feel guilty for stealing from the fucking *king*? Cunt's in a fucking coma, he's not missing any of the tax, and it's better off going to Red's girlfriends and their kids – but just because he couldn't bear the anticipation of it, of waiting for when he was going to get caught, and then the anticipation was gone and done and dusted.

And this is punishment enough – the fucking boredom of it, every day the same, no activity to take up your time except chat, books, and working the body in between working shifts. It's not what people think the punishment will be in prison, but it fucking is.

Caine often filters over to them in the course of his days ahead for all Red threatens him, and he seems decently at home with them, at home with Pike and Rosen and all.

Red's known this junior Pike a few years – he'd seen him about for years even before he'd taken on the smuggling jobs himself, and more than once on the outside, he and Pike had gone out for pints together, or at the least, Pike would find Red where he was at the bar and insist on paying for his drinks here and there, always flush with cash, though he'd make Red buy the first round.

"What do you think of him?" Pike asks now as Caine shuffles obediently off after Cornell to be escorted up to Villiers' house, laying his chin on his hand and watching thoughtfully as Caine's shadow disappears after the rest of him. "I bet he'd taste fucking great if it weren't for them cuffs."

"You like 'em with a bit of meat on them, don't you?" Red asks, and Pike laughs, laying his arm around Rosen's shoulder.

"Clearly," he says.

"Mind your tongue, or else you'll not be drinking from me again," says Rosen, flicking Pike's hand, but he's smiling all the while, and Pike chuckles, nipping at the shell of his ear.

"I'm waiting anyway," Pike says seductively. "Keeps you from getting anaemic."

"Prick," mutters Rosen, but he's gone from smiling now to grinning, and Red smiles at him.

He likes Rosen well enough – he'd come in a month before Pike had, and Red had stepped in to keep some of the lads on 10 from roughing him up for being a Jew. It's all very well roughing a lad up for having done something, it's another for doing it because he's had his cock clipped and says his prayers on Friday nights instead of Sunday mornings.

"He's lived a fucked-up life," Red says. "But you'd be hard-pressed finding a man in here that hadn't. I don't think he should be in here, anyway."

"Why not?" Rosen asks. "He did kill that man."

"Not on purpose," Red says, shrugging. "They only take a hard line on it 'cause they can't do anything until after someone gets hurts, lads like him, and they wish they could do it from the out. He's just another sort of vampire, really – he can't help the way he is."

"He can live without it," Pike points out, his hands twitching – he wants a cigarette, Red supposes, but he can't have one until tomorrow unless he wants to set off one of the fucking smoke detectors. "Then again, technically, so I can I."

"*Can* you?" Rosen asks, raising his eyebrows, and Red looks at him in surprise as well, but Pike shrugs his shoulders.

"Wouldn't be comfortable by any means, but I could probably get by on an iron-rich diet, a lot of raw and rare meat, shit like that. Vampirism is a bit different in a fae body than a human one – we get a bit more sustenance from magic than you sorts do, depending on the families we come from." Pike exhales the way he might if he had a cigarette to hand, blows out air and obviously doesn't find it quite satisfactory. "I think Caine did the best thing he could. Lived amongst mundies, worked with them – made sure anyone he might touch wouldn't be too affected by it in the event he sapped anything from them. That man reached for him, he said, touched him without thinking – some family friend or the like. He should have fucking remembered who he was, what touching the man would do to him."

"You'd think the guilt would be enough punishment," Rosen says quietly. "I think it'd kill me, that sort of guilt – to know I'd killed a man, a man I'd known, liked, loved, even. Without even realising it was him, without a cause. Without coming in here as well."

"You have enough guilt just by living, seems to me," Red says, and Rosen laughs, then comes over looking a bit more thoughtful, pensive.

"And him," he says quietly. "Him too."

* * *

Salvo receives his work duty after a few days in the prison – basic enchantment work. He has to sit an exam to show he knows how to write out the symbols, to show that he knows how to properly draw them or carve them into a piece of material. His cuffs remain in place, of course, and none of the prisoners are permitted to charge their enchantments themselves anyway to keep people from enchanting weapons or explosives – they simply lay out the runes and they're enchanted later, off the island.

Some of the prisoners are enchanting furniture and larger pieces of mechanism and machinery, but judging by how they talk to one another, how they chat, several of them were tradesmen or wizards on the outside – they're at home with magical plumbing and complex warding structures, some of them with licenses under their belts and specialist training. Salvo is not given anything so complex or large: he paints the enchantments into little gift items, charming welcome mats to clean off shoes, charming keys and small signs to create small lights, even enchanting a few toys here and there.

Every day is the same: he goes down to the prison for breakfast, eats, attends his work duty, eats lunch, finishes his work, has some free time, which he often spends reading or sitting quietly, listening to others talk. Generally, he gravitates toward Rufus Redford – he prefers "Red" to Rufus, and Salvo doesn't fault him that – and his friends: Callum Pike and Ira Rosen.

Red is a confident man, tall, square, fat, and thick with muscle – he's one of the tradesmen that works in enchantment, although he doesn't use precisely the same skills he had on the outside. He's a trained magical glazier, apprenticed when he was fourteen and left school early to take up the work – he's worked for years with huge panes of glass, fitted windows in all kinds of public buildings, even in some of the royal palaces, even in Camelot Castle itself – but here on the prison work detail he mostly enchants craftsman's tools or complex pieces of magical machinery, scaffolding, and things like that.

According to chatter around the prison, Red is in on tax fraud on a large scale, and a lot of organised theft that he'd done through his work, never doing the stealing himself, but organising for others to do it – Salvo gets the impression that he and Pike were already familiar with one another before meeting in prison.

Pike is in for some violent convictions – not murder, mostly aggravated assault and battery charges – alongside a long history of drug trafficking offences, and has been inside for short stretches twice before; like Red, Rosen is in prison for the first time, although Rosen's sentence is a good deal shorter.

Rosen's only going to be inside for another twelve to eighteen months – Red has close to a decade left on his sentence.

"How long you got?" he asks one afternoon at lunch, and Salvo looks up from his plate to meet Red's brown-eyed gaze. He has a few scars on his face, and on the backs of his hands – one, on his forehead and cutting through his eyebrow, is from an enchantment he messed up when he was scarcely eighteen, the pane of glass exploding outwards and the shard only narrowly missing his eye.

Rosen and Pike aren't paying attention, engaging in a very flirtatious game that Salvo can't determine the precise rules of, but seems to involve a lot of trying to finger one another's wrists while kicking each other under the table.

"Six years," Salvo answers.

"That's a long time for an accident," Red says disapprovingly. "Half my sentence, that, and I did what I did on purpose."

"No one died from what you did," Salvo points out, and Red sighs, shaking his head. "The point was that I was irresponsible, I think. That I should have taken better precaution, should have worn cuffs like these."

"They hurt, don't they?" Red asks, raising his eyebrows, and when Salvo doesn't say anything, he says, "I've seen a lot of mages wear those – here inside, sure, but in my line of work too, seen cloistered mages have cuffs like that, to keep them from going mad from the amount of magic around them, or to keep them from harming others. One thing to wear them for a quick outing outward, or to opt into wearing them out of some fucked up religious sadomasochism – one man's torture is another man's kink and all that – but it's another to wear them every day just to fucking live, isn't it?"

Salvo looks back at him, and then asks, "Is this you showing compassion for my perspective, the better to catch me by surprise when you turn on me?"

"And when am I gonna get the opportunity to turn on you, when you're Villiers' special little lad?" Red asks dryly, tilting his head and looking back at him with his lips twisted in a grin. He's got uneven teeth – his jaw's slightly uneven, Salvo thinks, from when he boxed as a teenager and a young man – and Salvo finds that he likes that. He likes how they look, like how much his teeth show his expression when he smiles. "Follow you back to the old man's house after dark?"

"Don't tell me *you*'re jealous of the warden's special attention," Salvo says.

"Something tells me I'm not his type," Red says.

Salvo wonders what Red would say, if Salvo told him. If Salvo told him Villiers hasn't touched him yet, nor seemed even to want to – if Salvo told him that he sleeps in his own very comfortable bed, in his own room, that Villiers barely even sees him most days, let alone speaks to him, with him.

Most nights, he's escorted back to Villiers' house by a guard, doesn't walk back with Villiers at all, and Villiers has already retired to his office or his own bedroom for the evening. Would Red believe him, if Salvo said that Villiers hasn't touched him yet, and he's not sure the old man ever will? Does Salvo even believe the latter part himself?

"Does he frighten you?" Salvo asks.

"Villiers?"

"Yes."

"He's a frightening man," Red says. "Scary sonuvabitch, he is."

"You're a good deal bigger than he is," Salvo points out. "He hasn't a size advantage on you as he might on me – quite the opposite, in fact. And he's elderly, and... infirm."

"That the word he used?" Red asks wryly, insightful in a way that Salvo might like, if he let himself like men much –if he let himself like anyone who wasn't a mundie, any longer. "*Infirm?*" When Salvo doesn't reply, Red says, "He likes that people think of him that way, people that don't know what he is, don't have an idea of who he is. He might be crippled by that stroke of his, but that doesn't make him any less fucking lethal. It's injured dogs that'll harm you the worst, when it comes down to it. They've got less to lose."

"Only when you have them cornered," Salvo replies, setting his fork down on his plate. "An injured dog is only a threat once you start trying to corral it – d'you really think the old man is dangerous to you now, here?"

"He knows who I am, knows my name, has my file, holds the key to my lock-up," Red says. "To everyone outside of this fucking place, I'm a bastard with a laundry list of things to punish me for, on an island far away from everybody – here, I'm nothing, and he's God."

Salvo considers this, considering too the fact that Villiers is more his god than Red's, has more power over him – has even more privacy to do to Salvo as he pleases than he might Red, where there at least are, if not other prisoners as witnesses, there are other guards. Salvo has nothing, alone in Villiers' house with him, but his word and Villiers' own.

"I'm an atheist," decides Salvo, and that makes Red laugh – he has a good laugh, barking, sort of rough and throaty – before he turns back to the others to talk to them.

On Thursdays, the allotted day of his prisoner number, Salvo goes into the prison library and withdraws three books – the limit – and throughout the week returns them through the slot before waiting impatiently for his opportunity to retrieve new books. After six months of good behaviour, he'll be able to take out six.

He has no one to call on to transfer money to him for the commissary, and he's on a long waiting list for a prisoner assistance program on the mainland to get back to his letter to see about transferring some money from his own accounts, so he doesn't buy anything there – the prisoner wages for their labour are low, though not as low as they are in mundie prisons, he's fairly certain. A day's labour can actually buy you *something*, anyway, so the wait isn't the end of the world.

"You have a very fine hand," Villiers remarks one Thursday evening as they walk back to Villiers' lodge together. It's raining, but the rain isn't especially heavy, just falls in a very fine mist that sticks to his hair and the back of his neck and his hands. He's carrying his books inside the leather satchel Villiers had handed him for the purpose, to keep them from getting wet. "I examined your handiwork from today. How long has it been since last you pursued enchantment?"

"Not so long," Salvo murmurs. "I used to whittle when I was a child – it was supposed to hone my concentration, keep me calm, and keep me practising enchantment when I had to go to mundie schools. I wasn't very good at animals – I was a bit better at architecture, at carving lighthouses, cabins, castles, towers. Enchantment was a bit more concentrated still, carving very small figures in place – I'd carve buildings and make them light up, make windmills turn, water flow, similar to the kind of stuff I'm doing now."

"Those skills will serve you well here," Villiers says. "Would that schools were upfront about what education will best serve a young person when they're inevitably incarcerated."

"Inevitably?" Salvo asks, and Villiers makes a quiet, amused sound.

"Something of an inevitability with you, young man," he says, and the two of them step into the corridor, Villiers leading Salvo not to the bedroom that serves as his cell but through to a small sitting room, some armchairs beside a fire, a chess table set up and waiting. "Do you play?"

"Not really," Salvo says. "I whittled some sets, but never liked to use them."

"I've never been much of a man for the game myself," Villiers says, sinking into one of the armchairs and gesturing with one long-fingered hand for Salvo to take the other seat, which Salvo does. This is only the third time he and Villiers have sat down together once they're in the house – the first time, when Villiers had first brought him up here, a cold night a week back where Villiers had invited him to read beside the fire where it was warmer than in his room, and now. "It's the sort of thing expected of a man my age, a penchant for chess games and long hours whiled away with a broadsheet newspaper."

"You must resent it," Salvo says as he picks up a pawn and moves it forward. "Getting old – being disabled."

"Of course I resent it," Villiers says mildly, moving a knight. "You would resent it too, and will do, as you grow older – you chose to remain intact, after all, no matter the risk it posed others. You only accepted this condition of chronic pain when it was forced upon you. Age forces such things upon us all."

Salvo says nothing, reaching forward for the next piece. "You were an assassin, before. That's what they say about you."

"I was," Villiers says, his lips twitching. "Although outside of a blunt and straightforward place like this, various polite epithets are applied to the profession instead – attaché, intelligence agent. I served the crown a good many years – from the age of fifteen onwards."

Salvo frowns, furrowing his brow. It's one thing for a man to be apprenticed as a glazier as a teenager – as an assassin seems a bit much. "What, you were in the army?"

"I was enrolled in a private school," Villiers says. "A military school in Scotland, Sons of Cumhaill. I was born in London, not in a particularly affluent area, but I earned a scholarship as a young boy, and boarded from then onwards. Sons of Cumhaill, upon its founding a millennium back, was originally a school for the children of knights and high-ranking battle mages, or for titled youths in need of blooding before they might lead their family lines. The reason for dispatching one's children there has changed, but much of the syllabus remains the same – training in traditional weapons, battle magic, poisons and venoms, battle tactics, and so on, alongside a rather robust focus in other valuable subjects. History, literature and culture, magical sciences, languages, politics, economics..." He gestures vaguely with his weaker hand – he can't lift the arm as high as he can his other, and the hand is a little limper on the wrist than seems entirely right, the fingers unable to complete the easy movement the ones on his other hand can. "A feeder school today for the army, for certain areas of the civil service, for the Knights' Circle."

"Wow," Salvo says, and he's unable to hold back his curiosity as he looks repeatedly between the board and Villiers' face. Villiers isn't as old as those he'd worked with in the care facility, many of whom were in the later stages of dementia or struggling with other debilitating and degenerative conditions, but he'd always enjoyed the aspect of the job that concerned making conversation, listening to older, wiser people talk about their lives.

Salvo's never been an adventurous sort and doubts he ever will be, lacks the natural appetite for such things, but despite not being very interesting himself, he's always enjoyed showing interest in other people, talking to them.

"Wow?" Villiers repeats, arching his eyebrows, the very word coming out dripping with irony, not fitting his accent and his careful enunciation. "Does it truly seem so lofty?"

"Maybe a bit. Are you, um…" Salvo doesn't know how to ask the question exactly as he moves his bishop. "How posh are you, exactly? Like, for you to get this scholarship, you've got a posh accent, but is that… yours, or did they train it into you?"

Villiers laughs. It's a reserved laugh, compared to how some men laugh, his head turned to the side, and Salvo is fascinated at the stillness on one side of his face versus the other, the way the paralysed muscles can't mirror those on the other side. He likes it, actually, sees a strange sort of handsomeness in it like he does in Red's uneven teeth and jaw – like in some art, where people use asymmetry.

"I'm not as posh as I sound, no, though it's too ingrained in me now to be an affectation," Villiers says. "My father was a mundie, a drunk, who walked out on my mother. In her youth, she was a dancer, a performer, and then became a teacher of the sciences. She developed a magical intolerance after an injury, had to carefully measure her direct exposure to active magic and enchantment, so we lived in a non-magical area of town."

"I knew a girl like that," Salvo says. "Hers was part of an immune condition, but we went to the same magical therapy centre – for her, it was regular controlled exposure to help her body not go overboard with the allergic stuff, for me, I was meant to be trying to train in my power."

"She had more success than you did, I hope."

"I think a bit more," Salvo murmurs, shrugging. "They tried her with a fleshturner, to see if they could reach in and basically just make her nervous system a bit less sensitive, but that didn't work, and then they tried different steroids and stuff. When we were really young, you'd see she was sick with it, like she'd have hives and stuff always, and her skin was really bad – for me, going through puberty made my problem much worse, but for her, I think it really helped and made it more manageable."

"These conditions aren't as well-understood, and thus aren't as predictable, as we would often like," Villiers says, shrugging his shoulders.

"Were you resistant to magical treatment for the stroke? Same genetics?"

Villiers looks mildly surprised, and Salvo likes that look, as well, likes the slight wideness of his eyes, the way he leans in just slightly. "Quite right," he says softly, and his gaze roves now over Salvo's body, over his chest, his neck, before back up to his face. Salvo feels warm, and he wishes it was just arousal, wishes it was just him wanting to fuck the old man, but Villiers isn't exactly his usual type, older, thinner, angular.

The hunger he's feeling, the intimacy he wants, is... different.

"To return to my anecdote, it was nineteen eighty-three, two days after my birthday. My mother had sent me the new David Bowie on vinyl, and I snuck away from evening rec to listen to it up in the music tower. We weren't meant to go up unaccompanied, cretins that we were, all of us, liable to damage instruments or try to dangle one another out of the window."

Salvo blinks, trying to imagine it, Villiers, angular and awkward limbs in the way of a teenager, upside-down with some other boy gripping his ankles. "You got dangled out of a window?"

"More of a dangler of boys than a danglee by them, for my sins," says Villiers, and Salvo hears himself laugh. When he moves his pawn, Villiers is quick to take it – so quick that their fingers brush against one another.

Villiers' demeanour might be naturally cold and flat, but his fingers are warm, and Salvo feels the bone-deep ache inside his guts, the craving to get these bracelets off him and soak that warmth and the life that powers it into himself. Ever since poor Brownie died underneath him, ever since he felt the crackle of his magic into his fingertips, he's hungered for it, *wanted* it. He'd never tasted it before – the power had been latent until he'd started puberty, and it had been weak at first. He'd sapped a little from people, but not enough to hurt them, just to make them a little tired and drawn. About the same time as he'd had a significant growth spurt, when he'd gotten taller and started to gain more weight and muscle, his absorption rate had changed too.

Augmented – significantly.

Overnight, it had gone from something of a joke, an unfortunate side effect of his company, even a party trick from time to time, to a genuine risk to everybody around him, with no choice in the matter.

"So you listened to the record?" Salvo asks, and Villiers exhales.

"Not that night, no. His majesty, the king regent, was sitting at the music room's piano when I made it up the stairs."

Salvo doesn't know that he'd be able to cope with it if he went out somewhere and came back to Myrddin Wyllt sat in front of him, or any knight, or any kind of famous person, really. He's never really felt at home with fame and influence. "Would have figured him for the drums."

Villiers chuckles. They're each making their moves fairly quickly, black and white pieces lining up on each side of the board.

"And what, he asked you to kill someone?"

"Wanted me to kill the music teacher, in fact."

"So you did it?"

"Gladly – I'd never liked him much, and he hated David Bowie."

"Is that why the crown wanted him dead?"

"No, he was a spy, apparently," Villiers says, although he frowns as he says it, furrowing his brow. "Something like that, anyway – you may well think ill of me, young man, but I didn't ask many questions. A very attractive and powerful mage was offering me money and his permission – his approval, even – to kill a man in cold blood. I was hungry for the chance, and quite eager for it."

There's something chilling in how easily Villiers says it. Salvo couldn't even call it a confession, he doesn't think, because there is no implication of regret or shame, no play at secrecy or modesty – he says it openly and with a remembered relish, and his tongue comes out from his mouth to wet his lower lip. Salvo looks down at his knees, trying to make sense, or to somehow organise, the tumultuous emotions tumbling over one another inside him – the craving and the hunger and the desperate, greedy want; the shame and the horror and the disgust at the fact that he wants it; the faint wish that it was a regular lust, a normal person's lust and desire; the jealousy at the ease Villiers finds, for being the sort of person he is.

"You didn't..." he starts, and the question goes dry and dusty on his tongue.

"Hm?"

"You don't sound guilty," Salvo says. "You don't sound— you *killed* him. And you talk about it like it was easy, like you always, like you always wanted it. Didn't you have, don't you have a conscience?"

"No," says Villiers smugly, making his move. "I've never been burdened with such a thing. Since I was very young, what I craved, what I wanted, was blood, death, feeling another man's life in my hands, and having the power and the privilege to snuff it out."

Salvo feels a mix of sick and desperately, almost painfully hungry. His fingers twitch as he looks out over his pieces, at where Villiers has moved his king to. "Do you think it would be a burden, if you'd had one?"

"It burdens you, doesn't it?" Villiers asks snidely.

"Check," Salvo says, moving his queen, and Villiers looks critically down at the board, then sighs with a lopsided smile that genuinely is quite handsome, Salvo thinks.

He considers what it might be like to kiss the old man, wonders what it would feel like, if he'd be able to feel the weakness on one side of his mouth rather than the other – and then all of a sudden he imagines the rest, imagines that it might be like to sap the magic out of him through his mouth, imagines feeling that hot, desperate tingle in his own lips, in his tongue, sinking down his throat and suffusing him. He imagines the electric, overwhelming thrill of it all, imagines that hot, giddy flow of someone else's power in him, someone else's *life* in him.

He hasn't kissed anybody on the mouth since he was fifteen himself, at the same age Villiers was killing a man, and back then the magic had been just a warm tingle against his lips, a sort of heady rush around his ears and heating his face – he knows what the real thing feels like, now, knows what it feels like to sap the force from the whole of someone's body, to be suffused with stolen energy. He knows what it feels to have someone else's soul subsumed into his, and it's the best feeling in the universe, and he hates himself for wanting to taste it again.

"You dastardly little thing," Villiers says, not without pleasure or satisfaction as he takes the head of his king under his fingertip and tips it over. "You set quite the little trap for me, didn't you?"

Salvo smiles faintly. "You're bored here," he says quietly. "With the prisoners, with... this."

"Often, yes," Villiers agrees.

Salvo studies him for a few moments, and there's a distant ache inside him, a faint compassion that pangs against the inside of his rib cage. Is Warden Villiers spared that as well, the same as he is a conscience? "Why work here as a warden, if it's so boring, if you want for company so badly that you're taking a prisoner out of the main lot and bringing him here to lose to him at chess?"

"It's quite simple," says Villiers in mild tones, and then he moves so quickly that Salvo almost doesn't see him, that he's not cognizant of what's happening until Villiers is on top of him. The older man's weight is incandescently warm in Salvo's lap, straddling his thighs and pinning him back in the winged back armchair, and half of his cane has been drawn back from the rest, showing the blade sheathed inside it.

Salvo can't breathe, can barely even think with the heat of Villiers in his lap, his bony knees digging in against the sides of Salvo's thighs, and compared to the warmth of the older man's body, the blade of his secret sword feels very cold against the underside of Salvo's chin.

He feels dizzy, because he's terrified, certain that Villiers is about to slit his throat, is about to bleed all the life out of him for *real*, no metaphor and no magic about it. Villiers' expression is cold and haughty and he smells of a subtle cologne, one that's just a little bit sweet, makes Salvo want to lean in for more of it. Red was right. An atheist he may be, but here is Villiers demonstrating how godly he is, how absolute his power is over Salvo here, without witnesses, without an audience, without any protection at all.

Paradoxically, as frightened as he is, there's arousal too, heat sinking down and tingling between his legs, heat between his thighs.

"I have complete authority over each and every one of you," Villiers says in a very quiet whisper, and Salvo breathes in very carefully through his nostrils, but when he swallows, an involuntary reaction, he feels the twitch of the blade against the skin, probably cutting off one or two hairs. "I could kill you right here, young man, and little fuss would be made of it, the paperwork mine to draw up – it isn't morality or fear of surveillance that keeps me from bringing you into my bed, chaining you to it, if I wished to."

"And when my sentence was up?" Salvo asks faintly, feeling dizzy, and Villiers laughs. "Would they ask where I was, to have me released?"

"Such terrible behaviour," he says faux-seriously, pouting out his lips and stroking the thumb of his bad hand, mostly limp, against Salvo's chin. It still feels as warm as the other, even if he can't move it as well. "We had to add a few years to your sentence."

"Oh," says Salvo. He wonders what Villiers would say, if he was to tell him that he and Red used the same words as one another, describing Villiers' position. He wondered if Red and Villiers have had this conversation before. "You— Why did you have to stop being an assassin, when you can still *move* like that?"

"You're very good at flattery, boy, did you know that?" Villiers asks, tilting his head to the side and looking more than a little amused, his lopsided smile almost indulgent now. With his good hand, this time – it only takes the flick of a wrist to put his blade back into its sheath and set the cane aside – he spreads his hand on Salvo's chest to brace himself, then eases himself up and out of his lap, onto his feet again.

Maybe it's just because it's not as fast, but this movement is a little clumsier, and Villiers has to be careful about which side he's putting his weight on, has to lean his good hand on the chair to steady himself as he stands, and then gets his cane beneath him again.

"I'm not good at flattery," Salvo says. "I'm not really good at socialising, to be honest – I was okay when I was working, talking to people, letting them talk, trying to make them feel good, make them feel safe, make them feel human even though they were sick, or disabled, or just really, really tired, and in a lot of pain. But I've not been able to go out, basically, since..."

"The core of effective flattery is always the appearance of sincerity," Villiers says mildly. "Being truly sincere is just another way to go about it, I suppose. You don't seem very frightened for a man who's just had a blade held to his throat."

"My life's in your hands either way," Salvo says, adjusting himself subtly in his seat, because his cock is hard and it's not as well-hidden in his loose prison tracksuit trousers as he'd like. He tries to shift the head of his cock against his waistband to keep it from pressing forward too much, but the way that Villiers' eyes flicker downwards makes it clear it doesn't matter how subtle he makes his erection appear. "The blade was just an example."

"Quite right, of course," Villiers says, and then the blade is bared again, and this time the very tip of it is resting on his shoulder, the silver of polished metal catching the light. Salvo stares down at it, at how sharp it looks, and very carefully, very slowly, glancing up at Villiers – for what? Permission? Approval? Just to see the older man's face *not* change? – he touches his finger to the side of the blade and immediately draws it back with a quiet hiss.

"Thought it would be blunt, did you?"

"Not really," Salvo says, and tries to make sense of the multiple wants and lusts inside him, the way they tangle with one another, the way they twist about each other like vines. There's something almost like a whine, almost like a moue, in his voice – which he doesn't let out on purpose – as he asks, "You're really not going to fuck me?"

"Never," promises Villiers, and he slides the blade in closer, drags the tip over the line of Salvo's collarbones through his clothes before it comes to rest in the hollow of them. "If I pierced here, through this little hole in the bones, useful little target on a thinner boy like you, I could cut right through your trachea. You'd aspirate on blood, unable to draw oxygen into your lungs, and what leaked out of you would froth and bubble."

Salvo's cock gives a desperate twitch between his legs, and he doesn't make a noise, but it shows in his face, he thinks – Villiers laughs at him, and makes a show of sheathing his blade his time, sliding it back into its place with a quiet *shkkt* of noise.

"What a curious boy you are," Villiers says. "Satisfy my curiosity, won't you – would you rather I kill you, right here, enjoy the powerful eroticism of a cruel and nasty bastard like me threatening you just like this, perhaps with my boot against that precious little cocklet of yours for you to grind against," (now Salvo *does* let out a helpless, embarrassing noise, and his trackies feel a little bit wet at the pre that dribbles from the head of his prick), "or would you rather slake your thirst and drink all there is from me? Sate that hunger of yours, gorge yourself on my magic until I'm dry?"

"You're part of the way intolerant to magic, you said," Salvo says to avoid the question, although he's so full of want that his prick *throbs* – he'd been horny after drinking poor Brownie dry, no matter that the man was never attractive to him, a friend of his dad's. He'd been stunned on the floor in the street, Brownie laid out and pale and still and going cold beside him on the cobbles, and for all his fear and horror and guilt, at the same time he'd felt blessed and beautiful warmth and satisfaction and satiation… and his cock had been the hardest it had ever fucking been, on the verge of coming even as the mage cop had come to cuff him, even as the magical police had cordoned off the area and taken away his corpse, and begun to take his details down.

The high hadn't dissipated for hours, until he was alone in his cell, and only then had he felt cold enough to start sobbing over what he'd done.

"You might not even make a good meal," he adds.

"Perhaps not," Villiers allows. "But any sustenance at all is nectar to the starving man, isn't it?"

"I'm going to go to sleep now," Salvo says, getting to his feet.

"Go to bed, at least," Villiers says dryly.

The door hasn't even had time to lock behind him before Salvo has his hand around his cock to pull desperately on it, to get himself off.

* * *

Later that week – a Tuesday – Salvo is caught as he makes his way to his work detail, grappled and hauled into a cell, and he tries to shout out a protest, call for help, but a palm is already pressed tight over his mouth. He's terrified of it, obviously, terrified, and yet a part of him sings for how much he's being touched, how the hands are grabbing at him, at his thighs, around his waist, up at his shoulders, even though the hands touching him are a bit clammy.

"Where *have* you been going at night, eh, you pretty little muzzled pup?" asks the voice in his ear, and Salvo doesn't recognise it, tries to raise his frantic eyes to get a glimpse at whoever it is in the cell mirror, but they've obviously smashed it and had it taken away. There's a gap on the wall where the mirror is meant to be, a different colour to the rest, and while there's newspaper bits pinned up, some animated pin-ups of actresses and models, Salvo can't glean anything from them.

He tries to squeal out a protest as a shoelace is strung through the gaps in his cuffs and used to hang his wrists over his head, up over one of the top bunk's posts, but this bloke is obviously old hat at this, keeps his palm pressed fast against Salvo's lips. He's dragging down Salvo's bottoms with his hooking thumb and his hand is a little cold and clammy where it slides down between his arse cheeks, thumbing at his dry rim, and he whimpers, but he can barely hear it, jolting when the same hand squeezes his bollocks and plays over his soft cock. He retches against the bastard's palm, but nothing comes up.

He's at the wrong angle, his arms behind him and hooked above his head, his shoulders wrenching and feeling like they might well be dislocated any moment. His don't tear up but he can feel the blood rushing through his veins, feel the adrenaline pumping, and he tries to kick, but it's painful to let his shoulders take any of his weight in this position.

"Think I'm getting the first go, aren't I?" asks the man behind him. "Haven't heard anybody else bragging about it, and I know everyone'd be crowing at having had the privilege."

"Let him go, Mason," drawls a Brummie accent from behind them, and Salvo looks desperately back at Callum Pike standing there, Rosen hovering behind him like a wide-eyed shadow.

"Fuck off, Pike," hisses Mason – Daf Mason, he guesses, the ex-miner in for rape who was in the papers, and Salvo watches Pike make a big show of sighing and adjusting his sleeves.

Where Rosen is small and round, plumper than Salvo is, and has sort of anxious, eager movements, often seeming like he's vibrating from the inside, Pike is often inhumanly still. It's not do to with being a vampire, Salvo doesn't think, but maybe more to do with his being part-fae, or maybe just personal to him – when Pike goes still you can't even see him breathing, barely see him blink, and that's how he settles whenever he's not talking or playing a game.

Or whenever, *he* would say, he's watching birds, or watching animals.

He looks like his dad, people say, some northern mob man who's famous enough for people to know what he looks like, not that Salvo's ever heard of him, though people say his dad doesn't do stillness like Callum Pike does. He's big and tall, lanky with a runner's muscle on him, and he does parkour, apparently – people have said that the reason he goes inhumanly, inorganically still like that is because he blends in with the gargoyles when he climbs tall buildings, but Salvo doesn't know that he believes that.

Pike isn't still now: he moves as fast as the warden had the other night, is nothing more than a flickering blue before Salvo's eyes, and then the weight of Mason behind him is gone, and he hears the other man groan.

Rosen has to climb up on the lower bunk to reach and undo Salvo's bindings – the double knotted lacing is deceptively hard to snap, even without Salvo being hung at a painful angle, but Rosen undoes the messy knot with quick, skilled fingers.

Salvo rubs at his sore shoulders as he stands up straight and turns to look at Mason. Pike has him sat on the floor, leaning back against Pike's chest, looking like a spider with a fly what with how long his legs and arms are contrasted with Mason's stouter, more contained form. Mason's eyes are glassy and his body has gone limp, and Pike is wiping his mouth with the inside of his wrist as he pulls back from the bloodied marks on the juncture of his shoulder, where he'd dragged back the man's shirt to sink his teeth in.

Releasing his grip on Mason's shirt collar, the bite is hidden as the fabric snaps back, and Pike drops Mason unceremoniously to the ground with a dull thump as he gets to his feet.

"You alright, Caine?" he asks casually.

"Yeah," Salvo says. "Prick." He kicks Mason hard in the ribs, and Mason's so out of it with Pike's vampiric venom that he doesn't even jump, though he does groan quietly after a second's delay. "Thank you."

"Thank Ira," says Pike, nodding to Rosen who – seemingly out of reflex – is rifling through the top drawer of Mason's side table. "I didn't hear you, I was sucking off Lee Havers down the hall."

"Sucking off his neck, or...?"

"His cock," Pike says helpfully, and Salvo huffs out a quiet laugh.

"Thank you," he says as Rosen comes away from Mason's things looking mildly disappointed. "You didn't really think he might have the keys to some kind of vehicle?"

"I suppose not," Rosen admits immediately, and Salvo feels his lips twitch into a tired smile as Pike laughs, gripping the back of Rosen's neck in that effortlessly easy, possessive way he does, squeezing. "A man does live in hope – I just forget, I suppose, where I am." He sighs, full of soft yearning. "I won't be able to get my hands on a *vehicle* until I'm out again."

"Did they take away your license?"

Rosen lets out a dismissive noise and waves a hand. "Never had one."

Salvo's pleased to have read him right, but as he trails after the two of them he looks at Pike's hand on Rosen's neck, wonders what it feels like. Vampires' skin is cold, he's heard – heard Rosen good-naturedly complain about it, even, but what would it feel like, the energy of him?

Pike splits off from them, loping back down the corridor to finish off Lee Havers, Salvo guesses, and he and Rosen fall into step beside one another.

"You on enchantment detail as well?" he asks. "I've not seen you in the workshop."

"No, no," says Rosen. "Embroidery, me."

"Embroidery?" Salvo repeats. He'd said when he was going through the list of work options that he sewed at school, and the guard doing his assessment had actually laughed and told him no, that he wouldn't be able for the sort of needlework they did here. He's even peered into the room where they're at it on his way back, and he's never noticed Rosen in there, but the guy's usually late for everything – who he *has* seen at work are very, very old fae, the ones that don't speak English and won't make any effort to learn, the ones that simmer with magic he can feel even with the cuffs on, that make his mouth water and his vision swim.

"Yeah, thanks to my granny, it's seven faeries older than sin and then me. They're nice enough, even if they try to use Hebrew with me sometimes and end up mixing it up with fucking Aramaic, not to mention that as you can imagine, their idea of Jews is, uh, a little old-fashioned. Fuck, it's *ancient*-fashioned. Do you know when someone's bigotry's so out of date you can't really even be that offended by it? I can't do enchantment – too dyslexic – and I can't sit still long enough to do some of the other crafts stuff. You can't get bored doing this kind of sewing, though, 'cause you have to work in sync with one another and go *fast*, layer magically charged threads over one another, the fabrics, all that."

"You like it?"

"Not really," Rosen says, "but it's better than bouncing off the walls, I suppose. Does he fuck you?"

Salvo looks sideways at Rosen, who looks politely interested, but if he thinks he's asked something rude, he doesn't seem worried about it.

"Villiers?"

"Yeah," says Rosen.

"No," says Salvo, more to see how Rosen reacts than because he thinks he'll really believe it – he's only young, really young, about twenty, twenty-one. "Why, would you fuck him?"

"Probably not," Rosen says, shrugging. "I think his face is creepy, the way his mouth droops on one side, and I don't like how he talks."

"His accent?"

"No, the, uh, what is it, a slur? From the stroke."

"A slur, yeah," says Salvo. "Though it's rather mild, I expect it was much worse in the recent aftermath."

"I don't really like old guys," Rosen says. "I've fucked them, obviously, to get my hands in their pockets for their keys or their phones, but I wouldn't fuck them for the sake of it. No offence if you like to fuck old guys, it's just not my thing."

"None taken," says Salvo. "I don't really have that much experience."

"What, you're a virgin?"

"Not quite, but I'm basically celibate," Salvo says.

"'Cause you'd kill people by fucking them?"

"Not mundies," says Salvo.

"Why not fuck mundies then?" Rosen asks. They're lingering in the corridor now, and Salvo knows he might be late for his own work detail, but Rosen obviously doesn't care – he's teetering back and forth from his heels to his toes, looking up at him with astonishing, kind of unsettling attentiveness. "Is it like, you can't be open with them or whatever?"

"I don't know," Salvo says. "I worked a lot, and I would be tired, and I tried a few times, um... Apps. Or going to bars. And I just wasn't good enough at it to make it happen, to actually get a guy to come home with me, or take me home, and it'd be months or years in between me actually trying, because it was just... It was excruciating. I don't know why. It made me feel horrible."

"Shame?" Rosen asks. "Do you hate your body?"

"Um," Salvo says. "I don't think so. Why, do you hate yours?"

"Sometimes," Rosen says, with the same incredible frankness with which he asks questions, and Salvo actually feels breathless with it. "Sometimes I only really feel okay 'cause I'm behind the wheel of something, and then it's like that's my body instead of this. All this flesh – not just 'cause I'm fat, but I guess that's part of it. All my family used to pinch at me, at my cheeks, my arms, anywhere you could pinch, really. You can't pinch metal or fibreglass, and even if someone tries, you don't feel it – and you're going too fast for them to try anyway." Rosen laughs, a scattershot sound that matches perfectly with his rapid fire, kind of clumsy way of speaking, but there's something about the laugh that doesn't match up with how he talks, a sort of tonal disconnect. "Anyway," he says, and instead of saying "bye" or "see you later", he just turns on his heel and walks away.

Salvo rubs the back of his neck, smiling faintly, and goes to work himself.

It was good to talk to Rosen right after – it's twenty minutes later that he remembers Daf Mason nearly fucking raped him, and then he throws up in the workshop sink.

* * *

Red walks with the lad back to the main block after they're done working. He'd asked if the lad was ill, but he'd dismissed both the guard looking over him and Red, and then just worked in even more palpable silence than usual. He's never chatty during his work detail, but at least he'll sit closer to other people and smile or laugh along with the conversation going on, listen more attentively if someone tries to give him advice, whatever else.

Most of today he's in his own fucking world, and he'd barely eaten anything at lunch, had mostly just sat there with his tray in front of him, barely touching what was on it before drifting back to work.

"You need to eat something," Red says behind him when they're in the queue. "Just get the rice if you can't stand to taste anything, but get a full portion."

Reluctantly, Caine takes a bowl of rice, half-heartedly putting some boiled carrots in it at the last minute, and he sits and eats in silence across from Red at the table until Rosen and Pike come to join them.

"You feeling okay?" Rosen asks, and then adds, "Start to sink in, did it?"

"Yeah," Salvo says hoarsely.

"Mason tried to fuck him this morning," Pike says when Red doesn't say anything, but looks across at them askance. "Had him trussed up when Ira got me to come in and rescue him. Speaking of, it seems my consequence for that has arrived."

"Fuck's sake, Pike," growls Cornell as he stalks across the bar, and Pike is stone-still as the guard grabs him by the collar and drags him up from his untouched tray. "You could have fucking *killed* him."

"I've never killed a man in my life," Pike says unconvincingly as Cornell hauls him away, and Red watches as Caine half-stands to his feet, looking like he wants to protest.

"Because he helped me?" Caine asks, looking horrified. "What are they going to do to him?"

"Solitary for a few days," Rosen says. "It's not like they can take his fangs out."

"Or cuff them," says Red.

Caine looks even greener now than he had earlier, but after a little quiet coaxing from Rosen he does sink down onto the bench again, and he reluctantly begins to eat again.

"They've put him in solitary before," Rosen says. "It's not as though it bothers him any. He wouldn't have stepped in if he wasn't willing to make the trade-off, a few days of extra boredom in exchange for stopping Mason raping you. You've never been raped before, have you? I don't recommend it, you're better off without."

That makes Caine blink a few times, not seeming to quite make sense of Rosen's tone. Even before he'd been brought to the nick, he'd known more than a few lads with personalities like his — more than a few lads who'd had blows to the head like Rosen had had as a lad and all, the sort of head injury that douses out a man's impulse control like a fucking church candle, and makes him talk like bullet fire.

Surely, working with old folks and the demented, he'll have met people that talk a bit more frankly than others, but unless you knew already, he supposes, you'd never know Rosen had an extra impact on him one way or the other. He's said to Red that he was always more impulsive than his siblings even before he took a brick to the side of the skull, and that you never know what's natural and what's from concussion.

Daf Mason's a victim of repeated concussion and all, though he's the more traditional headcase, Red thinks, the one that people might imagine. Angry, and a raper.

"I know I'm better without it," Caine says slowly. "Just— Just that it's not right, Pike being punished for stepping in in my defence. I'll talk to Warden Villiers about it."

"Oh, do you think maybe if you offer to suck him off or something, he'll let Pike out early?"

Red can see that initially Caine is just straight up taken aback by it, by the way that Rosen just comes right the fuck out and says it, but then he sees the wires connect and cross in Caine's head, the way he connects the idea of Villiers shoving his cock into Caine's throat with wherever Daf was gonna shove his earlier, and Red grabs Rosen's already-empty bowl from in front of him and slides it in front of Caine to catch the bulk of the vomit.

"Oh," says Rosen, not without sympathy, and pats his shoulder, which makes Caine, in a flop sweat under his tracksuit, jump and shudder, and then lean into the delicate squeeze of Rosen's pretty little hand. "Oh, it's okay. Villiers will probably take it out worse on Mason anyway – what with you being his special case and that."

Caine retches harder, and Rosen makes a face but awkwardly exchanges his now-full bowl for one another lad passes them from the next table over.

"Oi! Guard!" Red shouts over his shoulder. "One of you screws come be of some fucking use, would ya? Bring a mop and all!"

* * *

"He was only helping me," Salvo says for the third time, feeling out of sorts and strangely unbalanced, because he's in his bed and has a blanket over him, a glass of water next to another glass of flat lemonade on the bedside table next to him, a slice of very thinly buttered toast on the plate beside it. It has a few bites taken out of it, but more than half of the slice is still left – Villiers had stood over him and ordered him to take each bite, ordered him to chew, to swallow, to take a sip of water to ease it down, at the same time he confined him to his bed. "Warden Villiers, *please*, he only—"

"I understand your protest implicitly, Mr Caine, you need not repeat yourself again," Villiers says coolly. His cane is hooked on the back of Salvo's desk chair, and the man himself is leaning back against Salvo's desk, looking down at him in his bed.

He hadn't fainted, fully, but he'd been so stressed and sweaty and nauseous from throwing up on top of barely eating all day that his knees had gone weak when the guards had gotten him up, and Villiers had ordered him up to the house immediately.

"Mr Pike is under express instruction, as all vampires in this prison are," Villers says, "not to bite his fellow inmates. A vampire cannot be easily milked of their venom because they typically produce it too quickly, and Mr Pike, like so many of his unfortunate provenance, has rather powerful venom in any case. Were Mr Mason a diabetic, or otherwise under the weight of some condition that makes him particularly vulnerable to such venom, Pike might have killed him as easily and quickly as having snapped his neck. He is given a measure of blood each week to sustain his appetites, and he isn't to augment that diet."

"He drinks from other inmates during sex," Salvo mutters, reaching reluctantly for his lemonade and taking a sip of it. He'd felt fucking wretched, watching Villiers drizzle a little sugar into the glass and make it fizzle, stirring it until all the carbonation was gone, "that it not spur on your nausea any further".

"He isn't to do that either," says Villiers, his arms crossed over his chest. You'd not know one was weak, with him supporting them like this against his breast like this. Salvo doesn't really understand why it bothers Rosen so much, the slur – it's so mild, you'd easily think it was just from his posh accent rather than from the stroke. "Although he's good enough not to render his willing cohorts fit for the infirmary. Intimate contact between inmates is *itself* prohibited, I might remind you, but regardless of how Pike penetrates his cohorts – or indeed, is penetrated by them – we avoid official evidence of the fact so long as his partners are not hospitalised."

"And what about Mason?" Salvo asks bitterly, putting the glass down on the coaster before reaching reluctantly for the toast and forcing himself to take a bite of it, to chew it, to swallow it down. It's cold, and it feels too thick and heavy in his mouth, and he hates it, but he sees Villiers incline his head slightly in visible approval, and he doesn't hate that.

It's the only thing today after Mason, except for Rosen babbling at him when he'd forgotten about it, that he hasn't hated completely.

"Dafydd Mason is recovered from his stupefaction, and will be fine come morning, I've no doubt."

"He tried to rape me," Salvo says. "He tied me up and he stripped my trackies off me and he was going to rape me. He touched me. He touched my—" He squeezes his eyes shut as he feels his stomach turn over, trying to swallow down the nausea, feeling the toast wanting to come back up on him.

"More lemonade," Villiers orders, and Salvo's hand trembles a bit as he drops the plate in his lap and picks up the lemonade, swallowing a bit more down. He thinks the sweetness of it will make him gag, but it overwhelms the nausea, actually, the acidity of it and the sugar at once, and it fucking annoys him, actually, because Villiers is looking at him kind of smugly from his place on the other side of the room. "Why did you not call for a guard?"

"He had his hand over my mouth," Salvo says. "He grabbed me in the corridor and pulled me in, and as he tied me up and stripped me and— He had his hand over my mouth the whole time. I couldn't say a thing, I was making noise but no one could hear except Ira, who went and got Pike."

"Who pulled Mason off you, knocking him out with his bite, yes?"

"Yeah."

"And then?"

Salvo stares at him. "What do you mean, and then?"

"You didn't call for a guard then," Villiers says. "You left Mason on the floor of his cell, a puddle of drool collecting under his gaping jaw, and took the effort to bruise one of his ribs before you left him there."

"How'd you know it was me did that?" Salvo asks, looking at his plate instead of meeting the older man's eyes. "Not Pike? Or Ira?"

"Mr Rosen is not violent – to the point of pathology, he avoids violence, in fact, though I must say his vegetarianism makes providing healthy and satisfying kosher meals rather easier whilst avoiding potential interference from other inmates, so I suppose I ought render no judgement on it. And had Mr Pike kicked Mason in the ribs, he would have broken one, not just left a bruise."

"I don't like you," says Salvo, and Villiers laughs richly and quietly, supporting his weak arm with his other as he unfolds them, and then leaning back further against the desk, rolling his shoulders.

"I'm wounded, I'm sure," he murmurs. "You did not call for a guard, young man. Mason was not discovered until two hours after, and he could easily have died. Mr Pike would be spending more than three days in a solitary cell had he brought *that* about, I must say."

"So? He'd just tried to fucking rape me," mutters Salvo, tearing into the toast with his fingers 」and finding that it's strangely cathartic, tearing it in half, so he tears it into quarters, and then eights, and then tries to tear it into sixteenths, but mostly by this point he just has crumbs all over his hands and on the plate and a little bit on the sheets. "Why the fuck should I have called for a guard?"

"You forgot, didn't you?" Villiers asks, arching an eyebrow. "I know that Mr Rosen likely did as soon as he left the room. He's forgotten his shoes more than once before whilst wandering the halls – his sewing companions consider him quite the queer little thing."

"Maybe *Pike* forgot."

"Mr Pike is well-familiar with the drill, by this point. He didn't forget a thing."

Salvo glares at him, and Villiers smirks his cold, lopsided smirk. "It didn't occur to me," he admits, shaking out his crumby hands and putting the plate back on the counter, and Villiers walks forward and takes hold of the top sheet in his good hand, supporting himself on the side table with his weaker elbow and sweeping the sheet back with a surprising speed and strength, letting out a sound like a sail filling with a gust of wind. He shakes out all the crumbs before he passes it back, and Salvo smooths it over himself.

"You were never a nurse," he says.

"Never," Villiers agrees. "I've always been rather more comfortable ushering someone toward death rather than out of its clutches."

"You'd be handfeeding me if you could," Salvo accuses him. "Would have brought in the plate and glasses, would have tucked me into bed. Bet you've tampered with an IV – have you ever put one in?"

"No," Villiers says softly.

He's standing very close, now, leaning on the end table instead of the desk – he's so much closer, and it's more intimate, like this. Salvo has to lie back on his pillows and look up at him, and it's even more unequal, even more imbalanced, the dynamic between the two of them. Salvo can't stand the idea of touching himself, not at the moment, but there's heat between his legs, and his cock is half-hard even before he breathes in the sweet scent of Villiers' cologne, and he loves it, craves it. He wants to bury his face against Villiers' belly and feel the touch of his warm, slim fingers in Salvo's hair, touching his fingertips against his scalp, wants Villiers to hold Salvo's body to his.

"We're not meant to put them in, care assistants – we're not trained for it," Salvo murmurs. "Not accredited, anyway, and you're meant to be. Inserting IVs and taking them out, that's an invasive procedure – I got sent on a training course to take and process blood samples, but I should never have been doing IVs or catheters. Understaffing being what it is, though, if I wasn't doing it, or one of us doing it, there'd have been a Hell of a wait, sometimes, so they just showed us, and taught us how, and unless we were getting inspected, it was..." Salvo exhales, tapping his fingers against the sheet, against his knees. "It's delicate work, the tourniquet, the needle, finding the vein. There's so much power in it. There's so much, um, vulnerability in it. It's just this portal right to their insides, to their heart. You can put anything in it – too much medicine, too little. Insulin to really fuck somebody up, but not even that, though. All you really need is a little bubble of air."

"You needn't inform *me* of that," Villiers says softly. "As I said, I'm more familiar with those latter points than I would be any actual nursing."

"That's what I mean, though," Salvo says. "I always wanted to help people, care for people, yeah. I always craved it, I always... My dad had a pacemaker put in, and two different women on my street were nurses, and one of them minded me after school, and that was even without all the check-ups I had to have, as a child, the extra attention. I liked it. I liked the way nurses talked, and I liked how people paid attention to them and how they gave instructions and orders and help and I liked how physical it was, the, the knowledge. Like they could go into a cupboard and look at all this equipment, all these weird little devices or bits of tubing or whatever else, and just know how to use all of it to help you, to heal you, to fix you. But it was the power of that, really. I've always felt a bit bad about it, but it's not like you're going to judge me, like you're going to fucking care. I liked nursing because it was *authority*

– more authority than a doctor, sometimes. You never hear the doctor going, "Actually, nurse," and correcting what they've said, but nurses are always stepping in when the doctor's fucked up."

He looks up at Villiers, whose expression is not so obvious in its smirk now, but whose attention is fixed on Salvo's face, studying him intently.

"You'd like to be feeding me," Salvo says. "You'd like to be bringing the glass to my mouth instead of trusting me to do it myself – you'd like to force each bite, each mouthful of water or lemonade. You'd massage my throat to make me swallow, even, if you had the chance."

"Teasing me with such seductive talk will not convince me to release Mr Pike any earlier, young man," Villiers says, his voice a little bit hoarser, a little more resonance in it. Arousal, that is, arousal, and want. Salvo swallows.

"What *will* it get me?" Salvo asks, and Villiers laughs quietly, then picks up the plate with his good hand and walks away.

"Go to sleep," Villiers orders him. "No work detail for you tomorrow – you can take your choice of confinement here, or in my office."

"How cold is your office?"

"Quite."

"Here, then."

"As you will," Villiers says, and after setting the plate down in the corridor, he pulls the door shut behind him.

* * *

Caine doesn't come down from the warden's house at all that day. The screws won't say anything about what's up with him, but when Red asks Kim Adder, he says that there was a little dispensation, that he was confined to bedrest in his own quarters, but was noted down on the infirmary log as being unwell.

Not much of a surprise, that.

"Hello, Red," says Rosen when Red steps out from the workshop, and Red raises his eyebrows at the sight of the lad, reaching out and touching his knuckles to the back of Rosen's forehead, because he's pink all over, and sweating.

"Seems like *you're* red," he mutters. "The fuck happened to you, you jog down the corridor?"

"Oh, there was a fight in the embroidery hall," Rosen says, reaching up and wiping his face with his sleeve. "I had to run – the old faeries can do all sorts to each other, but it'd fuck me up, I'm not two thousand years old and with skin as thick as tree bark. The magic that would give them a little burn would go right through me."

"Right," Red says, raising his eyebrows, but he puts his hands in his pockets and walks alongside Rosen down the corridor, toward the canteen. Rosen hadn't eaten lunch with Red – he'd been chattering away with some recent new transplant who's in from London for arson, and is apparently an old schoolmate of his. "D'you mind if I ask you something?"

"No," says Rosen.

"Why're you in a magical nick, not a mundie one? Was it a magical train you tried driving off?"

"Not that I got caught, but they knew I had done," Rosen says mildly. "And they decided they couldn't trust me not to blab away to mundies and not keep secrets – I'm no good at keeping secrets."

"Fair enough," Red says. "That what had those old tree fuckers going mad at each other? You blabbing secrets?"

"Didn't fully follow a lot of the conversation, to be honest, I normally don't," Rosen says. "The way those old pricks talk to each other is fucking *weird* – it's not just the language they use, I've kind of been starting to pick up some of the, um, I think it's too old to even be Welsh, it's some kind of Brythonic. But they talk in verse and riddles and stuff with each other, so even if I can make out the words or recognise names and things they're saying, it's well beyond me to understand what they actually *mean*. They were doing some sort of poetry thing today, a bit, um... I don't know, they were roasting each other. Something about someone's daughter, maybe? And fucking her? I don't know. But old Bleiddgwn flipped his fucking lid, and he was properly screaming at Cadllew, and they were already angry at each other, and then Toutorixs said something else, like, commenting, or a joke, and then they were all trying to rip each other to shreds. I had to run out, and then French had to flip that switch, you know the one that locks the room down and chokes all the magic out? They'll be in there for days until they're either calm enough to come out or until they fall into hibernation, so either way, I don't have work detail for a while."

Red blinks a few times, because it takes him a little while to actually comprehend that Rosen's stopped talking – how the fuck he makes sense of what those ancient cunts are saying, let alone what the protocol is around them, he has no idea. Most of the inmates keep a *wide* berth from the prisoners that have been imprisoned at his majesty's pleasure long before this prison island was even built, and have sentences that last centuries or millennia instead of being decades at the most, for their own fucking safety, not to mention their own sanity.

"Hibernation?" he repeats. "What, like fucking bears?"

"If they're starved of magic for long enough, yeah," Rosen says evenly. "But apparently they normally tire themselves out fighting and arguing before they get to that point. Fingers crossed, though! I wouldn't be able to embroider on my own, so they'd have me doing something else. No Caine today?"

"Apparently he's ill," Red says.

"Oh, right, okay," Rosen says, and furrows his brow. "Yeah."

"You want to help me with a job after dinner?" Red asks, and Rosen lights up.

He doesn't ask for any details at all, of course, before he says, "Sure!"

It's not like Red wants him doing anything particularly risky in any case – Rosen chats up a fucking storm to the trustee mopping the floors in the infirmary, the doctor's already gone off for the evening, and Red knows that the infirmary nurse, a little prick called Julian with eyebrow piercings, will be off getting high at this time of day.

All he wants is to pay Daf Mason a little social call – and funny enough, he doesn't find the prick in situ.

"Is there a reason yourself and Mr Rosen are wandering the corridors with no-doubt pilfered sets of keys?" Warden Villiers asks in withering tones, and Red straightens up, his hands behind his back.

Rosen's eyes widen, his lips parting, and he says anxiously, his gaze flitting back and forth, "Erm, hello, Warden, uh, we're not, we haven't been, I'm—"

"Don't trouble yourself attempting deception, young man, we both know it beyond your capabilities," Villiers advises, and Rosen blows out air from plump lips, and he looks reluctantly at Villiers' outstretched good hand, palm up, before he drops the tools from his pocket into the warden's grasp – a bobby pin and two half-melted embroidery needles. "Mr French said you weren't injured in this afternoon's fracas between your fellow needleworkers. He is correct, I hope?"

"Yessir."

"Why were you loitering about the infirmary, then?"

"Where's Salvo Caine?" Red asks, and Villiers' uncanny gaze flits to Red's face, his thin lips twitching. He's a scary cunt, and there's no mistaking that, but it's not like it's Red's first time dealing with scary academic-seeming types, the ones with more power and danger simmering under the surface than you can see in their muscles or feel in their magical fields.

"Ill from yesterday's escapades, still," Villiers says.

"And Daf Mason?"

"Mr Mason?" Villiers repeats, and tilts his head to one side, then smiles a coolly satisfied smile. "You really thought Mr Pike would face punishment for stepping in, but Mr Mason would face no consequences for his actions at all?"

"Is he in solitary?" Rosen asks, and Villiers nods for Red to open up the door for them to go downstairs, which Red does, Rosen going ahead of him onto the landing.

"No," says Villiers, and shuts the door after them.

* * *

"Dress yourself for dinner, if you would," Villiers had said when he came back from the prison proper, and Salvo thinks about it when he shadows, plays it over and over in his head, turning it over. In Villiers' posh, stupid accent, made up and learned to make him scarier as an assassin or as a spy or whatever the fuck else, it sounds like it's a bigger thing than it actually is.

For dinner, like it's an occasion, like they're in some period drama, like he's gonna put on a tail coat and fancy trousers and nice shoes and a bowtie, and like there's gonna be all lords and ladies sitting down around the dining table and prawns in a dish and a butler pouring drinks.

He puts on his issued trackies, and a t-shirt, and his sweatshirt, and he walks out into the corridor through the unlocked door to his room and down toward the little sitting room where they ordinarily eat together, if they share a meal. It's never an inmate that serves them, not like how inmates work down in the kitchen – Salvo's actually never seen whoever it is that serves them in Villiers' house, and he's not sure if there's even a *person* doing it at all, or if it's all enchantment.

He knows that the place gets swept and cleaned – he tries to keep his room tidy because he's just that sort of man, but sometimes if he doesn't fully make his bed if he's in a hurry to go in the morning, or if he spills something on the desk or spills shampoo or something on the bathroom floor, it's always cleaned up by the time he's back. His sheets get changed once a week, and a lot of the time, he can see that someone's hoovered or scrubbed the floors or done something like that in the sitting room or in the hall.

Normally when Villiers calls him to come eat dinner, there are plates already on the little table for them, but there aren't tonight, and the chess board isn't laid out either.

"Ah, there you are," says Villiers, and he walks forward, sliding past Salvo and back into the corridor, then gesturing with two fingers for Salvo to follow him down the hallway, which Salvo does. "Feeling better, I hope?"

"Yeah," Salvo says. "I was a bit bored, to be honest. Finished all my books."

"Those Lawrence Kidd romances again?"

"Two of them," Salvo says. "The other one was an Agatha Christie. Where are we going?"

"Oh, through here," Villiers says in smooth, easy tones, and leads him through the door and into Villiers' home office. It's a much warmer affair than the one he has in the prison proper, a fire burning in the hearth, and there's a fancy brocade wallpaper on the wall. On the other wall is another door, this one slightly ajar, and Salvo peers through it, because that's Villiers' *bedroom*.

He has dark violet bedsheets made of cotton, not silky at all, and Salvo gets a glimpse of the brass bar beside the bed that's obviously there to help him up and down, and—

Villiers closes the door shut.

"Not what I brought you here for, young man," Villiers tells him, and limps across to his desk, where he slowly spins his chair around. It's a big, leather-backed thing, so that until it's turned around, Salvo can't see what's in it – who's in it.

His mouth goes dry as he looks at Daf Mason, his hands cuffed behind his back, his ankles chained together, a gag like a horse's bit stuffed in his mouth, forcing his teeth apart. Salvo stares at him, uncomprehending, unable to breathe, his heart beginning to speed in his chest, sweat beginning to gather on his skin, beading on his forehead.

His stomach clenches tightly like a squeezed balloon, and he's glad they haven't eaten dinner yet, glad that he was left with a plate of sandwiches for lunch that he ate before it was even one o'clock.

"What the fuck?" Salvo demands, the words coming out in a whisper, as if he's scared of Daf Mason hearing them. He's not really frightening, now that Salvo sees him like this – he's been thinking about him on and off today, trying to remember glimpses of him he's seen about the prison, thinking of him on the floor. He's not a big man, by any means – solid and stout, but not really *big*, not that intimidating. "What the fuck, Warden, you can't just—"

Villiers has stepped close to him, close enough that Salvo is distracted by the scent of his cologne, so distracted he doesn't realise that Villiers is reaching for him, touching him with his surprisingly warm fingers – so distracted he doesn't realise why Villiers is actually touching him until the cuffs fall aside, dropping into Villiers' hands, the left, then the right.

Salvo actually feels dizzy for a second, magic rushing through him like he's just been dropped into a river of magical flow, and he feels the hot bleed of it through his veins, under his skin, feels the incredible sing of pure energy in his head, between his ears, on his tongue, in his heart, his belly, in his very core. He whips back and steadies himself on a wall as he adjusts himself to it, his eyes closed tightly, his heart pounding.

It's like the world temporarily ceases to exist, like it's just him and all the magic around him instead, and it's surprisingly very intimate, feels good and comforting and warm. It's like magic itself is cradling him in its embrace, enfolding each of his limbs, cradling his body, stroking through his hair, even.

He'd forgotten.

Salvo had forgotten how good it felt, sometimes, all the magic in the world – he's been wondering of late how the fuck he used to manage it, how he used to stand it, not being touched, the awful skin hunger, the awful starvation in his muscles and in his flesh for other people touching him, not just for hugs or squeezes, not even for kisses or whatever else, but even just the casual touches of other people. Brushing shoulders with people in a corridor, feeling the weight of others in the crowd around you, wrestling, shaking hands, high-fiving, even.

Not like Mason's touch, no, not the grip of him, the violence of it, the fucking *invasion* of it, but everything else, everybody else.

The magic isn't a substitution, but it's good. It feels right, natural, satisfying, and he slowly breathes in through his nose, steadying himself and standing up straight as he looks across to Warden Villiers and Daf Mason.

He can feel the magic in the room. He never used to feel it much in the care home or in his own apartment – he could reach out and feel the electrical circuits sometimes, the flow of the wiring around his flat, separate from the concentrated magic in enchanted items of his own, in warded or enchanted furniture.

It had never been like *this*.

The whole of the island is singing beneath his feet, the soil rich with magical salts and proteins, magical root systems from trees and flowers, the ground rock heavy with magic from whenever this island was constructed a few millennia ago. He can feel every brick around him, taste on the air the order in which they were laid, can even imagine the ghosts of the men who'd laid those bricks – fae labourers, many of them, indentured to the crown for resisting the march of King Arthur's army.

He can feel the age of Villiers' huge, mahogany desk, feel the solid wood of it and the magic that gathers and settles in its grooves and secreted knots, in its enchanted brass knobs and handles; he can feel the enchantment on each of the furnishings and devices in the room, everything from the privacy charms on his in- and out-trays to the anti-pest ones stitched into the rug beneath their feet and inscribed on the bottom of his bookshelf.

He can taste them, all these magicks, discrete from one another, feel how scattered and chaotic the older magic feels, how untethered and sprawling it is; he can feel the straight lines and rhythms of the newer charms and enchantments, the magic channelled and controlled by careful inscriptions of symbols and writings; he can feel the *life* in it all, the energy.

Daf Mason burns brighter than the fire does.

Villiers does have a pulse to him, a font of magic buried in his chest and letting more magic flow through his body, but he's a lighter, less saturated grey where Mason is a hot burn of white energy, pure and wholly concentrated and radiating outward, and Salvo has never felt so incredibly and unspeakably hungry.

He can barely breathe, staring at Mason, unable to separate the detestable man in his vest and trackies and careful bondage, doused in a flop sweat and struggling helplessly against the leather seat beneath him, from the sweet fucking *nectar* that flows through him. Salvo can see it, feel it, taste it – magic gathers in the very core of a person, runs up and down their spinal column and out from their heart and their brain, flowing through the bulk of their nervous system and their arteries and capillaries, but Mason has been in magic all his life. Was raised in a magical home, learned enchantment as a child, worked in a magical mine, is now kept inmate in a magical prison, probably even raped magical victims – every ounce of magic in him, Salvo knows as intimately as he knows his own heartbeat.

Magic clings in caps around the tips of his fingers, where he's been enchanting all his life, and gloves his palms leaving gaps where the enchanted wooden heft of his pickaxe wasn't in contact with his skin; his hair and fingernails aren't as doused in magic as his skin is, seeming paler and less saturated than the rest of him; if Salvo stripped him naked and then stripped the top layer of skin off his back, he might even be able to read the old ghosts of the runes inscribed on the inside of his armoured mining vest, where the enchantment has left its ghost within Mason's body from so many decades of use.

Salvo's thighs touch Villiers' desk, and Salvo blinks, laying his hands on the wooden surface, staring down at it before he looks back at Mason. He hadn't even realised he was walking forward, hadn't realised he was even approaching him.

Daf Mason looks fucking terrified, tears on his cheeks, snot on his top lip and shining yellow in his stubble.

He looks at Villiers, who is watching him keenly, hungrily.

"You're letting me," he says, and his voice sounds strangely hollow in his own ears as he slowly moves around the desk, advancing closer. "You're— you're *letting* me? I can... There's so *much* in him, it..." He tries to remember what it felt like to be nauseous, but there's too much of a roar inside him to remember what the fuck something as awful as that felt like – he can't remember what it felt like to be nauseated and ashamed and horrible with Brownie's corpse on his conscience, and he can't remember either what it felt like to be terrified and scared and on the verge of throwing up at the memory of Mason's hands on his body, Mason's bondage holding him in place, the thread of Mason behind him. All he can feel, all he can really concentrate on, is the hunger, the need, and better than that, the knowledge of what the satiation will feel like, what wonder it will be to *taste* him. "It'll kill him," Salvo says weakly. He can barely hear that last part.

He can hear Mason's useless, pathetic begging, even through the gag in his mouth – he can't really make out the words, but he can hear his desperate fumbling in English and then in Welsh, which Salvo doesn't even speak. How many people have begged Mason like Salvo didn't have a chance to yesterday morning, have begged him not to hurt them, not to rape them, not to tie them up? How many people have plead for mercy and haven't had it from him, or haven't had the chance to do so because he gagged them first, like Villiers has gagged him?

"And what are you robbing him of, if you take his life?" Villiers asks in a silken voice that weaves around Salvo's heart and feels like it's making itself at home inside his skull, inside his heart, inside his fucking *soul*, and he likes it. He likes the sound of Villiers' voice, the taste of it. "The chance to ravish another unwilling party, to emasculate another prisoner? To bash in a fellow's brains, embarrass himself, be cruel, be ugly, be...?" Villiers trails off, and then gestures to the struggling, sweat-soaked Mason, pushes out his lips in a mocking pout, and Salvo looks at the slight weakness of his lips on one side of his mouth, and wonders what Villiers would do if he kissed him there, on that loose corner. "Look at him, Mr Caine," Villiers says. "Is it even the *moral* choice, to spare him?"

Salvo could touch Villiers instead.

He could reach out and grab Villiers instead, grab his wrists or his throat, touch his cheek, even kiss him – he could touch Villiers and sap from *him*, and show him exactly what he deserves, give him what he's asking Salvo to do to Mason...

But Mason burns so much brighter, and maybe he doesn't deserve it more – but Salvo deserves it more. He doesn't want revenge against Villiers, doesn't crave to take anything from Villiers, because Villiers has never taken anything from him.

He closes his hands around Mason's neck, moans aloud at the sudden shock of lightning-fast power crackling up through his palms ad up his arms, and Mason chokes and stiffens up and stops struggling and fidgeting all at once, frothing at the mouth as he chokes on air around the bit.

Oh, but it's ecstasy.

He can feel the stutter and shudder of Mason's swallowing throat under his thumbs, but it's nothing compared to the sensation of the feed, of the way all the magic gathered under Mason's skin, running through his veins and coiled about his bones, held in his every cell, transfers to Salvo instead. He feels as though he's flying, as though he's soaring, feels the rush in his ears, crackling over his skin, a whipcrack of wonder—

It's not like how it happened with Brownie.

With Brownie, he hadn't even known it was coming, had gone from nothing to everything in one moment and not truly been cognizant of what was happening, had never experienced the like of it before. He's more in control of himself this time, more attached to himself. He's aware of the moment that Mason's body, cold, his eyes dead, falls back in the chair, Salvo's hands releasing him.

Mason's cold sweat is clinging to his palms, and Salvo flexes his fingers, feeling the pulse of energy under his skin, and feeling strangely satisfied, strangely... whole. He stares down at his own hands as he clenches and stretches out his fingers, slowly rolling his head on his neck, his shoulders, his elbows, feeling oddly like a glass that's been filled to the brim, but not poured over.

He looks to Villiers, who is watching him intently, and he sees and feels the energy that runs through Villiers, too, the magic in the core of him and that flows through the conduits he's made up of, but what he doesn't feel, he finds, is hunger. Want, yes, desire – want for the older man to touch him, hold him, want him, but not to drink from him.

"I don't feel cold," Salvo says. It comes out in a soft and mystified whisper, and Villiers hums a sound of comprehension, or perhaps of understanding, or maybe just acknowledgement. He's holding out a tray, and Salvo obediently takes the two bracelets back off it, sliding them onto his wrists and clicking them into place.

It's as if the room goes suddenly dark again where before it had been drenched in light, his connection to the magical flows around him abruptly cut off by the enchantment in the cuffs, but he doesn't feel like *he's* drenched in darkness, doesn't feel as though he's been dropped into some dark pit.

He can feel his heart beating, is aware that his breaths are even, that his blood must be flowing through his veins, that his organs are at work.

"A hunger sated, yes," Villiers says. "I'm not surprised that warms you. Come, I have a bath run for you."

It almost doesn't occur to him that he *could* protest, let alone that he'd want to, as he follows after Villiers not, disappointingly, through to his own bedroom, but into the corridor and then to the master bathroom, which is very warm. A few candles are lit around the darkened room, and Salvo strips off his clothes as indicated, sinking then into the bath.

This is Villiers' own bathroom, more brass bars around the room to support him standing and moving, and Villiers draws over a brass-legged stool before stripping off his cardigan. He's wearing a dark brown wooden vest over his shirt underneath, and after hanging the cardigan up on the back of the bathroom door, Salvo watches as he rolls up the sleeve on his bad arm, and before he can start with the other, Salvo reaches out with his still dry hands and rolls it up for him. He neatly folds the shirt cuff up and over, trying to mimic the same angles Villiers had used on his other side, up to the elbow.

There are more scars on Villiers' forearms, the insides of his wrists and elbows – places where the hair on his skin has been burned or altered, marks where he'd been cut, even a messy, fatter wound that he thinks was maybe from a bullet, or was from something else with a straight path, like a sharp pike or stick.

Villiers keeps his weaker hand in his lap as he reaches for a glass jug and fills it from the water, pouring it over Salvo's head and wetting down his hair as he obediently tips his head forward. There are no bubbles in the bath, but it's fragranced with salts and smells faintly of flowers and a fruit, he thinks maybe peaches or apples.

"Your father was ill when you were growing up, you said, a pacemaker. Your mother?"

"She worked," Salvo mumbles, grateful for the curtain of hair hiding his face from Villiers' gaze. He doesn't feel any compunction about being naked in front of the other man – a part of him is frustrated that he's not looking at Salvo's body with any particular desire or hunger, but that doesn't sting so much feeling Villiers' hands on him, moving over his body.

"Who bathed you, as a child?" Villiers asks.

Salvo is quiet, leaning closer to Villiers' hands as he pours cool, creamy shampoo through Salvo's hair and massages it into the curls, squeezing and combing his fingers through to ensure he gets as much coverage as he can with his one working hand, the other remaining rested on his knees.

"Does your sapping effect impact a pacemaker?"

"Not as a matter of course," Salvo says. "I can, um, be aware of electrical fields and stuff, but I don't really impact them. But he had other stuff wrong with him, and he was ill a lot, and tired a lot. So he couldn't touch me much, because it'd take so much more out of him than someone else."

"And your mother?"

"She was already tired from work."

"And grandparents? Other family members?"

Salvo doesn't say anything, leaning his cheek into the gentle scrub of Villiers' narrow fingers as they rub behind and at the underside of his ears, massaging down the back of his neck. It feels good, sends thrills down his spine, and he likes how strong Villiers' approach to it is – he likes the authority with which Villiers moves his head one way and then the other, how he tilts Salvo's head for him to pour water over his scalp before smoothing it out.

"I suppose I can imagine it," Villiers says mildly. "Relatives sitting back from you, coaxing you and tutoring you through combing your hair, brushing your teeth, how best to wash yourself, not touching you and demonstrating as they ordinarily might for a small child. Were you aware of the casual touches your childhood was robbed of by your condition, hm? Cognizant of the way other parents and relatives reached out and touched children of the same age as you – stroked their hair, patted their cheeks, held their hands or gaze them affectionate squeezes and half-hugs? Did you understand why you were an island, even before you were old enough that your touch was a death sentence, and not a promise of mere discomfort and exhaustion?"

"They touched me at check-ups," Salvo says, although he doesn't know why he says it – is it a defence of his family, an excuse? An assurance he's not as stunted as Villiers must assume he is? An explanation about why he is the way he is about care? "Making sure I wasn't adversely affected by it, that I was still growing, that I was..."

"Were you a rich boy, of course, or from some more established magical family, your condition would have been treated very differently. You'd have been dispatched to a boarding school with as rich a magical field and history as they might find for you, appropriate sources of sustenance brought to you."

"Victims," Salvo says.

Villiers shrugs. "Perhaps. But were you trained from youth to control this need of yours, not to mention regularly fed, perhaps you wouldn't sap so strongly from those you touch. No boarder was suggested, no alternative school?"

"I didn't have the grades," Salvo says, vaguely remembering the way his mothers' smile had faded as she'd excitedly torn open the envelope with him watching, the way it had slowly dripped from her face and faded into the ether like evaporating steam.

"They wouldn't have seen you as having anything to offer, I suppose," Villiers says. "No money or storied blood, no especial academic or magical ability. Only a hungry mouth to feed, and to what benefit?"

Villiers massages conditioner into his hair, and then he has a washcloth in his hand and he's scrubbing in slow, rhythmic circles over his shoulders, his neck, the top of his chest, his arms, and then his belly, between his thighs. He's not remotely horny about it, isn't sexual about it, and Salvo's own arousal isn't actually that overwhelming, isn't as satisfying as the pure *intimacy* of it, and not just the warmth and comfort of Villiers' hand on his body, the scrub of the soap and the cloth and his fingers, but the control of it. He feels like he's just so much more hot water, like he's part of the bath he's stewing in, he's so relaxed, not having to think at all, not having to put any of his thoughts or feelings in order – all wants and needs and anything he might think about dissolve into the water as well, and all there is, all there needs to be, is Villiers' hand guiding Salvo's body to where he wants it, and then Villiers' hand making him clean.

"This is what I was talking about," Salvo says when Villiers reaches over and pulls out the plug of the bath on the chain. "The power of it, care. Complete authority."

"Indeed," Villiers murmurs, standing up and reaching for a towel from the heated rail. Salvo looks at it, the way he holds it out, obviously higher held in one hand than the other, looks at the tight clutch of his weaker hand around the lower corner of the towel, and Salvo stands up and steps onto the bath mat, exhaling as Villiers wraps the towel around him – and at the same time, wraps Salvo in his arms.

Salvo smells his cologne and smells the pomade he uses in his hair, feels the soft wool of his vest, feels the heat of Villiers' body.

"Do you think I'm pathetic?" Salvo asks.

"Hardly the correct question, young man," Villiers murmurs. His breath smells faintly of coffee, and looking up into his face, Salvo stares into the terrifying freeze of his icy blue eyes, their noses brushing against one another. "A more suitable question might be – if you *are* pitiable, as is your concern, is it pity I feel for you... or something else?"

Salvo feels like he's been drenched in hot water for a second time, searing over his flesh, and this time he *is* aroused, is keenly aware of the heat between his legs and the fact that his body is tight up against the warden's, and the warden's breath is intermingling with his, and is close enough to kiss.

"Take the towel from me, if you would," Villiers orders him quietly. "Bathing you I might attend to sitting down – drying you off would be a dangerous gamble against my ability to keep my balance."

"Sorry," Salvo says, taking the towel, and Villiers laughs.

"What on earth are you sorry for, stupid boy?" he asks, raising his eyebrows, and grips Salvo by the jaw and squeezes. It's not painful by any means, is a firm grip but a gentle punishment, and fuck, but he's hornier in this moment than he's ever been in his fucking life, Villiers laughing at him, holding him like this. "Do you want me to kiss you?"

Salvo's breath hitches in his throat, and he feels his lip quiver, leans forward. "Yes," he whispers.

Villiers leans in, gripping the side of the sink to better support himself as he does so, and their noses brush against one another again, and he can feel the heat of Villiers' breath as much as he can smell his coffee. He squeezes his eyes shut, waiting for Villiers' lips to touch his, but they don't – they glance over the side of his cheek, and then his breath is hot against the shell of Salvo's ear, and his knees go weak at the thrill it sends down his spine.

"Earn it, then," Villiers almost growls into his ear, and Salvo is humiliated by the fucking noise that squeaks out of his throat, involuntary and desperately eager. "Get yourself dry and return to your room, young man," Villiers tells him as he pulls away, throwing his cardigan over his shoulder as he grasps hold of his cane and opens up the door. "Your dinner should be waiting for you."

"Fuck me," Salvo mumbles, and Villiers laughs again.

"That, I will not do," he says, and limps off down the corridor.

* * *

When Caine is allowed back down from his special little holding cell up in Warden Villiers' house, whatever the fuck that looks like, he comes down with a smile on his face. It's a dreamy smile, distracted, and Red wonders if the lad's gonna be distracted from his work detail, but he isn't at all. He writes like a demon, moving a lot quicker through his little toys and small things than he normally ever does, carving runes into place or painting them onto wood panels with confidence and ease.

He's pleased to see Callum Pike and all, and when the four of them sit down to lunch together, Pike gives Caine a grin.

"What, you thought they'd fucking lock me away forever?" he asks.

"I just feel bad you were put in solitary on my account, that's all," Caine says.

"Where is he, Mason?" Pike asks, casting a look around the hall — it's a question Red's interested in hearing the answer to, and he looks at Caine's face for an answer, but his pretty brown eyes don't show any sign of guilt or regret. He, like Pike, casts a look around the room, tracing the lines of the long tables looking for Daf Mason's face. "You seen him about?"

"Went looking for him in the infirmary yesterday, but there was no sign of the prick. What'd you tell him, the warden?" Red asks, and Caine does look a little uncertain now, pressing his lips together and twisting his mouth just a little.

"I told him what happened, what Mason did," Caine says. "That it wasn't your fault, that you shouldn't be in solitary for defending me. But he didn't say anything about punishing Mason any extra, or putting *him* in solitary, or..." He looks down at the canteen table, nervously fingering the edge of his fork. His voice is very quiet as he asks, "Do you think he hurt him? Warden Villiers, do you think he hurt Mason in defence of me?"

"I bet it wasn't just to defend you," says Rosen pleasantly, patting Caine's hand in the most comforting way he's capable of. "I bet he goes looking around for excuses to kill people, sometimes. He probably gets bored that he's not allowed to any longer."

Caine stares at him blankly, seeming distantly horrified and not going exactly how the fuck to cope with that, and Pike laughs.

"You should come work with us when you're out," he says, reaching across the table and patting Rosen on the side of one plump cheek. "Sort of lads I could refer you to'd be more than happy to have you nicking cars and trucks for them."

"It's no wonder recidivism rates are so fucking high with you recruiting, lad," Red says, and he looks across at Caine, who slowly begins to eat his meal.

"I don't think my family would be very pleased if I became a drug-runner on top of stealing cars," Rosen says.

"Why not?" Pike asks. "My da's just another kind of florist, he and your da are two sides of a penny."

Rosen sniggers, and Caine looks across to him as he keeps eating from his plate.

"Your family are florists?" he asks.

"My dad and his two brothers, and a few cousins," Rosen says, nodding his head. "My mother's sort of the opposite – less of a green thumb, more of a death touch, you know. Liable to make a flower wilt just by touching it."

"I have something like that myself," Caine says, and Red stares at him – it takes Rosen and Pike a few moments for them to register that Caine's actually made a joke, especially given that the lad doesn't smile or grin or wink or do anything like that. Rosen laughs uproariously, tapping his little feet on the floor as Pike wheezes, slapping the side of the table, and Caine smiles a thin-edged smile, and seems to... Not get bigger, exactly, but fold out from himself a bit, not so small in his place.

"You never killed someone, before you killed that fella?" Pike asks.

"No," Caine says. "When I was small, it wasn't enough to harm anybody – make people tired, make them irritable, more than that. They wouldn't realise what it was, often enough, wouldn't realise why it was bothering them, if they touched me casually. I had to go to a mundie school – magical schools, even knowing what I was, teachers would touch me, lean on the back of my chair or tap me on the head or… And they'd start snapping, me gruff, annoyed. Like people who are ill, you know, it's not controllable. A history master nearly slapped me once for scratching a scab before he got hold of himself and remembered who he was, who I was. I never had that once I was in with mundies."

"I got slapped around at school," Pike says. "Mind you, it was normal back then."

"Why, when'd you leave school?" Rosen asks.

"I left early, I was fourteen, I think. '81."

"*'81?*" Rosen repeats, aghast. "So, what, you're *sixty-seven?*"

"Sixty-six," Pike corrects him, apparently offended. "Not sixty-seven 'til November."

"There was me thinking you were younger than me," Red says, laughing and shaking his head. "All the time you've said fucking *"age before beauty"* to me about buying the first round!"

"Well," Pike says, shrugging his shoulders. "You look it, don't you?"

Caine laughs at that hard enough to choke on his overcooked potatoes, and Rosen pats him hard on the back as he coughs and swallows down a mouthful of water to try to ease it down.

"I'll remember you fucking laughing at that, lad," Red promises him, injecting all the bass he can into his voice. "There may well be consequences."

Caine's eyes flash with a bit of energy, and as he wipes away the choking tears from his eyes and wipes his mouth with the back of his hand, he says, "Alright," with a note of challenge in his tone. "Consequence away, old man. How old are you, sixty-five?"

"You little prick," Red growls at him, half-laughing himself, but Caine only beams at him, all easy smiles.

Daf Mason doesn't turn up, in the next few days, but things get back to normal.

After another two days, the ancient fae that make up the rest of Rosen's fucking sewing circle tire themselves up, and Rosen reluctantly returns to his work detail instead of dossing about in his cell all day, although at least he stops complaining about being fucking bored when everyone else abandons him.

Caine keeps up the fast pace at work, often finishes up a little earlier than he used to, and one evening as Red finishes up for the day, he finds Caine lingering in the corridor outside of where they're embroidering. The door is slightly ajar, and Red swallows hard, clutching at his own chest to try to cope with the unholy fucking vibrations that sing through it.

He fucking hates it when the old fae sing together, the noise of it putting the fucking willies up him. They're all twice the size of most fae you'd see today, those old cunts, as tall as the trees they've sprung from with skin like tree bark, so that Rosen looks even smaller than usual when he's in there with them.

The sound radiates out from the embroidery workshop and into the corridor and right down the halls, bouncing off the tiled floors and the undecorated walls, and it makes Red's ribs feel like they're vibrating, and he feels it on the inside of his ribs, the inside of his skull, the inside of all of him.

It's a waulking song, or something like it, a song to keep them in rhythm with one another as they work, Red guesses, although when he hovers behind Caine and looks into the room over his shoulder, he sees that they're done working for the day. They're trying to teach Rosen the song, judging by how they're all sitting in their chairs and have their faces angled toward him, one of them moving fingers that look like tree roots in rhythm to keep Rosen on beat, and he's nodding along.

Red can't make out Rosen's voice in amongst the noise they're making, a collective sound louder than a choir of fucking thousands, louder than a church organ if you had your ear right to the pipes, and it should hurt, it's so fucking loud, but it doesn't hurt, exactly. What it does is make his bones feel like they're shivering, makes all his nerves fucking jangle, and he looks to Caine.

His expression is one of soft and quiet awe, his thumb tugging and playing repeatedly over one of the metal cuffs around his wrists, his lips parted, his eyes as big as fucking plates. When the fae stop – oh, God, fuck, it's like if *trees* could sing, it's like if they were singing right from the core of the fucking Earth – it's an unspeakable relief, and Red leans against the wall, exhaling.

One of the fae stands now, and he says something in his unearthly and ancient voice, the language guttural. Red's no big Welsh-speaker himself, but he can hear the ghost of the Welsh in it, he thinks, or the roots of it, although it sounds closer to fucking *Latin* to him.

"Um," says Rosen. "He said, um... Something like, asking if you're imagining what he tastes like?"

Caine smiles at the fae – Red can't even tell them apart, but he thinks this one is Toutorixs, because a crown of bramble thorns, complete with blooming white flowers, is sprouting around the crown of his tree-trunk head – and puts out his hand.

"Oh, erm, Salvo, they don't, they don't shake hands," Rosen starts to say urgently, but Toutorixs reaches out and winds his root-like fingers around Caine's outstretched fingers, around his palm, around the base of his wrist.

Caine gasps, but instead of pulling away or shouting out loud, he leans in closer, and his eyes shine gold for a moment, the cuffs around his wrists flashing so brightly they look ready to fucking melt, before the screw in charge of the embroidery crew, French, barks, "No contact between inmates, you know that! Stop— doing whatever you're doing!"

Toutorixs pulls back and lets out a gut-wrenching sound that must be a laugh, because all his friends join in, and Caine and Rosen follow after Red toward the canteen, Rosen soon beginning to chatter on about something or other – horse-racing, Red thinks, although he can't make himself tune into it properly, still trying to work that awful sound out of his head.

He's quiet as he eats, as quiet as Caine had been before – and just as quietly, apparently, Caine follows after him to his cell when he goes there instead of playing a game or watching TV or anything else.

"You're bottom bunk?" he asks softly as Red slides into his bed, which has two blankets on, one that Sandra had sent in for him when he complained about the winter chill his first year in, and another Patience-May had brought in when she'd visited for his birthday earlier that year, sewn together of all different flannel shirts she'd gotten from the scraps bag at work.

"Nah, Churn is more than young enough to jump up there himself without having me do it," Red says, and he watches as Caine steps slowly around the room, looking at Red's books and Churn's, looking at the pictures Churn has up on the wall of his daughters and his wife, and at the painted picture Sandra's daughter had sent in for Red of the flowers in their garden.

"You have children?" Caine asks.

"No," Red says. "But the women I take up with, some of their kids like me."

"Even though you're in prison?"

"They don't know the difference between me being in the nick and being away at work."

"I suppose not," Caine says, and toes off his shoes.

Red leans back in bed and lifts up the blanket, and the lad apparently needs no more invitation to slide between the blankets and in close, and Red exhales at the feeling of Caine's body warm and soft against his. He doesn't know what shampoo the warden's giving him in his house, but it smells very nice, of nectarines. When he slides his hands underneath the waistband of his tracksuit bottoms, he finds that the flesh of the lad's thighs and arse is just as generous as it looks, and he sinks his fingers into the warm yield of it, squeezes.

Caine sighs luxuriously, leaning in closer and burying his nose against Red's chest, banding his arms around Red's middle, and as Red keeps pressing and massaging at his buttocks and thighs, kneading at them like bread dough, he feels Caine's prick against his thigh, feels the lad grind against him.

"I hope you don't think I'm going to fuck you," Red murmurs into his curls, "unless you feel like going door-to-door down the corridor and seeing what you can trade for a tab of sildenafil."

"Is every man in this prison fucking impotent?" Caine asks in a grumble, although it sounds pretty fucking sleepy to Red, and Red laughs.

"Only the fucking old ones you keep throwing yourself at," Red tells him dryly, and he waits for the lad to argue with him, for him to debate, for him to keep grumbling, but he doesn't do any of that. Red keeps squeezing the flesh under his fingers, rubbing back and forth, and with his other hand he reaches up and combs lightly through his hair.

"Feels nice," Caine says quietly. "No one's ever touched me as much as since I came here."

"No touching between inmates, remember," Red tells him. "And I don't think the warden's meant to be touching you either."

Caine doesn't answer.

He's fast asleep, breathing quietly in and out, and Red enjoys the heat of him and the softness of him and the scent, too. Not like a woman, no, but almost like being at home with one, until one of the screws comes along to break them apart. He wouldn't mind fucking him, by any means – he might well ask one of the other lads about trading him something for his ED if Caine likes the sound of it – but this is nice on its own, just sitting here and soaking in the lad's heat, the magic of him.

Red closes his eyes and lets himself doze until Cornell comes along to get them out of bed again.

* * *

In the observation room that adjoins Warden Villiers' office, Salvo stands at the window and looks down over the canteen, where most of the long tables have been folded away for the evening, and a few of the lads are sat around, playing chess or basic boardgames, or reading books, or sitting around and watching TV.

It's frosted on one side, the glass, and he hadn't even realised it was an observation window – he doesn't think he ever realised it was actually a window at all, and wasn't just a big pane of frosted glass behind the metal balcony with emergency stairs coming down, separate to the wall.

Red is playing cards around a table with Rosen and Pike, and from this angle he looks to be a bigger man than he is, in contrast to Pike's gangling limbs and Rosen's round but confined little form, broad as he is. Salvo thinks of how warm he is, when he's under the blankets and pressed up against Red's broad, hairy breast, very different indeed to the warden's spindly but muscular form, all joints and flat, hard edges of muscle.

In the past few weeks, he's been touched so much.

Touched by the warden, not just when he'd given Salvo a bath a few weeks ago, but in the intervening period as well – reaching out to adjust his clothes or his hair, touching him as he passes him by in the house, brushing his hands as they play chess together. Once, yesterday, leaning over ostensibly to take the salt from the table at dinner, and taking the opportunity to breathe in Salvo's ear.

Touched by Rufus Redford, petted and touched here and there, touching or chucking his chin or his cheeks or the back of his neck, and where they've been able to sneak it without being told off by the guards, Salvo curled up to doze in bed with him, or sit with his head against his lap or his belly while the TV is on and it's deniable enough that Salvo is sat on the floor in front of the sofa or the bench.

Touched by others, too. Toutorixs, of course, had gripped his hand a few weeks ago and sent magic flooding through him even through the cuffs – they're no match for the old fae and how much magic flows through them, and the others of the ancient fae have made a game of it, Rosen seems to think, reaching out to touch him when he walks by, zapping him with bits of pure magic that ripple right through him, no matter that the guards bark at them whenever they catch him at it.

Other touches, too. Brushes in the corridor, standing in line, and on Wednesday, when they'd been outdoors for exercise, Pike had taught him some wrestling grapples and holds. His hands *are* cold, his palms rough, but it had still felt good, had made him feel somehow real, feeling the weight of Pike's thigh against his chest or his arms around his chest, or feeling the solid weight of Pike's body under his own as Salvo tried to keep him pinned or still – especially, the whole time, feeling Pike's laughter and Salvo's own running through both of their bodies.

"Feeling hungry?" the warden asks as he enters the room, and Salvo turns back to look at him as he approaches, his cane making only the tiniest noise on the ground, his footsteps utterly silent. Salvo can only make out the noise of the cane's grip against the floor because he's so used to listening for it by now. "Even with those would-be dryads supplementing your diet."

"I thought dryads were meant to be pretty young women," Salvo says.

"I'm sure they'd present themselves as such, if they felt like it," Villiers says dryly. "But that would rather lead to unwanted attention in a prison like this, as I'm sure, by now, you're aware."

"How do you keep them here? Aren't they too powerful?"

"They're kept in situ by something far more powerful in its command over them than bars or chains, young man. Each and every one of those ancient creatures is bound in place by his word and his vow, as recompense for whatever crime he committed."

"Words are more powerful for them, I suppose," Salvo murmurs. "Fae, more than us, I mean."

"Words are powerful even for the two of us, I should point out. My accent has been trimmed and clipped, that I appear to be that which I am not – you speak with a vocabulary and a formality that comes from reading stacks of books, no matter that you were never afforded a lofty education. We're each of us lucky in that way, aren't we just?"

The warden is warm behind him as he comes closer, and Salvo quietly exhales and leans half an inch backward, feeling today's pin-striped waistcoat against his back.

"I'm told you were dozing in Mr Redford's cell once again yesterday," the warden murmurs in his ear, and Salvo shivers at the warmth of his breath tickling over the lobe of it. "Has he fucked you yet?"

"He can't get it up without a pill," Salvo says. "Same as you."

"Vasodilators are contraindicated for previous victims of stroke, as I'm sure you know," Villiers says, his voice quiet but his tone amused, and Salvo can feel his smile against the back of his neck as he reaches past Salvo to rest his cane against the wall. "In any case, it isn't dysfunction that prevents me from fucking you, young man, but disinclination."

"Am I meant to believe you don't actually want to fuck me?" Salvo asks, feeling as though hot water is beginning to flow under his skin as Villiers tugs up Salvo's shirt with a finger and bands his weaker arm tightly around Salvo's middle. He opens up his hand, but he can't grip very well with it or easily manipulate his fingers – it's mostly with the strength of his elbow and his arm, and the tuck of his chin against Salvo's shoulder, that keeps him upright. "The way you touch me. The way you look at me."

"I've never found myself vulnerable to the siren's call of penetrative sex," Villiers says as, with his good hand, he slides his fingers up under Salvo's sweatshirt and plucks at one of his nipples with a graceful, artsy movement like he's playing a string on an instrument, and Salvo whimpers at the sudden sear of sensation it sends through his chest and rocketing down his spine. His cock is hard, and his knees threaten to go weak. "Ah ah," Villiers starts sternly. "You're the only thing holding me up, boy – keep those legs strong and solid, unless you want us both clattering to the floor."

"*You'll* clatter, maybe, being all bones," Salvo mutters, heat rising in his cheeks as he squeezes his eyes shut, feeling Villiers laugh against his neck, his thumb and forefinger teasing and tugging over his nipple. "Or shatter. What do you mean, *siren's call*? What, you're like, asexual?"

"A side, I believe is the modern parlance," Villiers says, and before Salvo can grumble about that, Villiers drags his teeth down the side of Salvo's neck, making him whine. His eyes shoot open, terrified for a second that everyone downstairs will be able to hear him through the glass, that even if they can't see his face, they'll see the two shadows of him and the warden, and know it's him, know what the warden's doing to him, that they'll be watching. "How does it feel, when those fae touch you? Comparable to your feast on the soul of Dafydd Mason?"

"I don't believe in souls," Salvo says breathlessly, then groans softly as Villiers plucks at his other nipple, flicks over the tip of it with his neatly-groomed nail, his other hand sliding slower and gripping at Salvo's hip. Villiers' hands are so warm and his fingers are so clever and it feels *good*. He tilts back his head, turning it to the side and moaning when Villiers shows his approval by licking a stripe up the side of his neck, nips the edge of his jaw, then the lower part of his ear.

It's not the same – it hadn't been the same. The way the fae touch him *tastes* different to when he'd touched Mason, for want of a better word – their magic is older, richer, comes more from inside them than it flows through and gathers in them as it does in human beings. Even through the cuffs, even at a glancing touch, it overwhelms his senses and the core of him, but it fills him and leaves him fizzing over with it.

Mason had... sated him. Wholly and entirely, and a little bit more than that, but it had felt natural, though perhaps he shouldn't think of it that way.

"Do they suspect his demise is down to you?" Villiers asks, sliding a hand up to grip the base of his throat as he bites down harder now on the side of Salvo's neck, as if *he's* some kind of fucking vampire instead of Salvo, and then Villiers shoves him forward, against the glass. He's able to put more of his weight on Salvo like this, his hand going from Salvo's neck down between his legs instead, his fingertip tugging at the ring of Salvo's arse and making him squeak out a sound. "Do they know you to be a killer twice over, and hungry to lay waste to a third victim?"

"No," Salvo groans, reaching clumsily back for Villiers, one hand reaching back to squeeze his narrow arse, making Villiers let out a short, sharp, breathless laugh. "Why, d'you think I should fucking advertise it?"

"Temper temper," Villiers says, and uses the waistband of Salvo's tracksuit bottoms to ease his way onto the floor, and Salvo stands up straight, whipping his head around to stare down at the older man aghast.

"You can't be on the fucking *floor*, what about your knees? Sir, you can't—"

"It's not as though I'll be down here long, is it?" Villiers retorts – that's all the warning Salvo gets before he licks a hot, wet stripe from the back of Salvo's bollocks up to his hole, and the sensation wrenches through him, right up his hard and aching, dripping cock. All of a sudden, he's coming, white spattering the frosted glass of the window in front of them, his eyes tearing up, and he tries to stop himself from going wholly limp, bracing himself on the bar.

He's breathing heavily, unable to catch his breath, somewhere between hotly satisfied and a little embarrassed.

"Told you so," says Villiers.

"Fuck off," Salvo says, and Villiers laughs.

"Help me up, would you?" Villiers asks. "I am so very old and very infirm, and my thoughtless young lover has abandoned me to the floor."

"I could *kick* you."

"I invite you to try." He really does, too – Salvo would never, *could* never, he doesn't think, but when he looks down at Villiers on the floor, braced on his better knee more than the weaker one, he sees that the old man is more than braced for it, that he's hungry for it, wants to scrabble with him, wants Salvo to try to hit him, just so that Villiers can pin him down to the floor instead.

"Not today," Salvo mutters, a little too flustered to actually sound at all stern, and offers the old man his arm to help him up – as soon as his knees don't feel so much like fucking jelly.

* * *

It's Rusk and French that grab him just before lights out and knock him out with something like fucking chloroform. They don't frog-march *him* up the fucking hill, and they don't let him make his own way either. He just wakes up in a leather chair in an even fancier office than Villiers has in the prison proper, his ankles tied together, his wrists cuffed behind his back, a gag in his mouth.

Red sits back in his seat, looking around the room, at the fancy floor-to-ceiling bookshelves filled with leather bound and gilt books, at the astronomy equipment next to the window, an astrolabe and an armillary sphere, and more shit he's seen in plenty of fancy offices like this one, but has never learned the name of. There's a fancy rug that's probably centuries old rolled out on the hardwood floors, and all the furniture is good, heavy, antique stuff, and he can feel the enchantment in all of it, feel how old the subtle magic is, even if he can't feel the age of the wood.

Up on one wall are a bunch of frames: Villiers in a line of other bureaucrats or maybe other assassins, receiving some kind of medal or award from the king regent; a portrait of a young Villiers alongside a severely featured but happy-looking woman he guesses must be his mother; a few calligraphed certificates covered in more bits of gilt and fancy ink for his various degrees, declaring him Guillaume Copernicus Villiers, BSc, MA, MSc, MMSc, PhD.

He's been in a lot of offices like these over the years, talking about how they're going to fix the windows, what sort of glass or framing would suit best the architecture and mimic the original style, what sort of enchantment they can put in, what carpenters and joiners, what masons, he's going to be working with.

He's never felt at *home* in them, exactly, but Red's gotten used to them, almost comfortable with them. He's learned the names of the old-fashioned astronomical equipment, or vintage navigational tools, or basic entomology and demonology, learned to recognise certain bits of taxidermy. He's learned the basics of these fancy posh cunts' hobbies and interests, so that he's more comfortable talking to the bastards, and they're more comfortable giving him a big fucking tip.

He never thought he'd die in an office like this one. Figures.

"Fuck off," says Salvo Caine as he crosses over the threshold, staring at Red in his chair, and Red marvels at the expression on his face, at the way he shoots a fierce glare at Villiers and seems very surprised at the fact that it's *Red*, but not surprised that it's fucking somebody.

Lied through his teeth about Daf Mason, and Red never even suspected he was lying.

Caine isn't wearing his bracelets, Red sees – when he casts about to look for them, he sees them on a tray next to Villiers, and Villiers himself who's standing up straight and wearing a fucking green and gold housecoat over his clothes, like some fella in a vintage advert, all settled in his pyjamas.

"You aren't hungry after all?" Villiers asks, gracefully arching an eyebrow.

"Not *him*," Caine hisses. "Not h— he has a *family*."

"I can assure you, he doesn't."

"He has women he goes to see, women who love him – kids who love him."

"And you?" Villiers asks in mild, dry tones, sounding for all the world like he's about ready to laugh in the lad's face. "Do *you* love him? This trafficker and embezzler, hm?"

"Easier to love him than a fucking, a murderer and a creep!"

"Maybe so," Villiers says, delicately shrugging his narrow shoulders. Keeping his weight braced on his cane, he holds out the tray with his other hand, Caine's cuffs rested on them. "By all means, then…"

Red looks up at Caine as he slowly approaches, his pretty hands held awkwardly in front of his belly. It's been nice, the past few weeks, having Caine in his bed, feeling the softness of him, the warmth of him, smelling the fancy scents the warden apparently bathes him in for his own fucking pleasure, it seems. Strangely, ridiculously, he wonders in the moment how Caine dresses himself when he's not in the nick, what scents he likes to wrap himself up in.

Caine's gaze lands on Red's face, and Red meets it. They've not been talking much, really, not about the things that matter, not about the things that catch in the chest or in the mind – if anything, Caine seems pretty content to be petted and played with more like a cat than a young man.

He's overheard him talking to Pike, though, once or twice, the past few weeks, about the hunger he feels, about the need inside him – he'd been downplaying it, obviously, if he'd fucking killed Daf Mason.

He doesn't struggle.

He's not fucking stupid – he knows damn well he won't be going anywhere, up here in the warden's office, tied up in his chair, the warden being an assassin with however many titles and qualifications after his name, the lad with a fucking death touch in front of him, not having his bracelets on. There's no sense in struggling, not now.

The only man with Red's life in his hands is Caine – and it's only in *his* hands because Villiers has put it there.

"I don't want to hurt him," Caine whispers to Villiers. "Why'd you fucking gag him? He's not like Mason."

"If you don't wish to sate that hunger gnawing in you, boy," says Villiers in tones as dry as dust, but again, the bastard is still visibly on the verge of fucking laughing, "by all means—"

Caine swallows as he comes closer, his hands up close to his chest as he meets Red's gaze, biting the inside of his pretty plump lips – Red's not even fucking kissed them. That's what he gets for beating around the bush, isn't it?

"Sorry, Red," says Caine, and then his hands are whipping out, and Red closes his eyes as tightly as he can so he doesn't feel it coming.

It doesn't come.

The tray clatters to the floor, the magic cuffs jangling before they hit the rug and go quiet, and Red opens one eye to see that Caine has one hand gripping at Villiers' hand and the other wrapped around his throat.

* * *

"Oh," says Salvo, because Villiers' skin is beautifully warm under his hands, as warm as it ever is, and he can feel the magical flow beneath the older man's skin, is cognizant of the glow of the other man compared to the rest of the room.

He'd noticed, before, that Villiers' magical glow was lessened compared to Mason's, and it's lessened compared to Red's. Some people have thicker skin than others, thicker skin or thinner veins, so that you don't see their blushes as much when the blood comes to the surface, and this is like that, he thinks. Villiers has magic in him, but it's deeper under the skin, harder to get at – like Pike or another vampire would be hard to cut or bite your teeth into, because their flesh is harder, denser.

"It might behove you to know," says Villiers, utterly unaffected by the touch of Salvo's hands against his skin, even as he turns his hand up to playfully tickle the underside of Salvo's wrist, "that apart from building up self-defence techniques and immunities to various poisons, I *was* trained to resist draws like yours as a matter of course."

"You fucking cunt," Salvo whispers, and Villiers laughs, his thumb sliding warm against Salvo's palm, pressing against it. It feels nice. Salvo's never been able to touch another magical person since he was a kid without killing them – and never without hurting them, without tainting their feelings for him.

He wants to stay angry, wants to stay pissed, but a part of him is sparking to life inside because Villiers is *touching* him, and it feels nice.

"You can't win every chess game, dear," Villiers says, and tugs Salvo's hand to enclose around Red's throat instead. "Checkmate."

Salvo sees Red's eyes bulge and his expression of relief explode into panic and fear and pain, hears his choking sound of terror, and he can't focus on compassion right now, because all that matters is the rush of Red's magic into his hand, into both his hands when he puts the other on Red's cheek, draws from him entirely.

He should feel terrible, should be beside himself with guilt, but he doesn't – it feels wonderful. It feels wonderful, feels *sublime*—

"Good man," says Villiers, and kisses his fucking cheek. "You're free to come for dinner whenever it suits you."

"Free, am I?" Salvo asks, and Villiers chuckles, patting his arse as he limps away.

"As much as you're *good*, young man," he says, and goes out into the corridor.

Red's body is already going cold, but the room is warm, and as he feels the pulsing spread of stolen magic all throughout his body, rippling under his skin, Salvo feels very warm as well.

FIN.

More from the Author

If you'd like to seek out more of my work, *Heart of Stone* is a full-length novel set in the 18th century, and is a slowburn slice-of-life romance between a vampire and his secretary, the vampire ADHD and the secretary autistic. It has a lot of humour and domestic elements throughout.

My most recent release, *Powder and Feathers*, is a long-form contemporary dark romance with a great many fantasy elements, featuring a fucked-up dynamic between a Fallen angel and a depressed artist he begins stalking in the park.

If you're interested in perusing more novella-length pieces and short stories, I publish a huge variety of short stories that are available on a subscription model from Patreon[1] or as part of your Medium[2] subscription!

I normally publish at least one new piece a week, whether that's short stories, longer form short stories like this one, serial updates for my chaptered works, or non-fiction pieces like essays and analyses.

My name is Johannes T. Evans on both sites.

My website: www.JohannesTEvans.com[3]

My Twitter: @JohannesTEvans[4]

And finally, if you'd like to get regular email updates from me, with media recommendations, links to my most recently published work, and other little announcements, you can sign up at www.buttondown.email/JohannesTEvans.

---

1. https://www.patreon.com/JohannesEvans

2. https://johannestevans.medium.com/directory-of-work-6291c6e102b9

3. http://www.JohannesTEvans.com

4. https://twitter.com/johannestevans